THE YOUNG REFUGEES

ESCAPE TO
Liechtenstein

ED DUNLOP

journeyforth®

Greenville, South Carolina

Library of Congress Cataloging-in-Publication Data
Dunlop, Ed, 1955-
 Escape to Liechtenstein / by Ed Dunlop.— Rev. ed.
  p. cm. — (The young refugees ; bk. 1)
Summary: Hans and Gretchen discover a young Jewish boy hiding
from Nazi troops and decide to assist him in his escape from Austria.
 ISBN 1-59166-013-0 (Perfect bound paperback : alk. paper)
 1. Holocaust, Jewish (1939-1945)—Juvenile fiction. 2. Jews—
Austria—History—Juvenile fiction. [1. Holocaust, Jewish (1939-
1945)—Fiction. 2. Jews—Austria—Fiction. 3. Righteous Gentiles
in the Holocaust—Fiction. 4. Austria—History—1938-1945—
Fiction. 5. Escapes—Fiction. 6. Christian life—Fiction.] I. Title.
 PZ7.D92135Es 2003
 [Fic]—dc22

                                    2003017226

Designed by Craig Oesterling
Page layout by Melissa Matos

Printed in the United States of America

ISBN 978-1-59166-013-2
eISBN 978-1-60682-920-2

15 14 13 12 11 10 9 8 7 6 5 4 3

Dedicated to Mr. Takamori and his fifth grade class. Thanks for the encouragement that you have been to me.

"And be ye kind one to another, tenderhearted, forgiving one another, even as God for Christ's sake hath forgiven you."
Ephesians 4:32

Contents

Introduction

Austria is a small country in central Europe famous for its beautiful mountain scenery, mirrorlike lakes, and thick, green forests. This beautiful land, slightly smaller in area than the state of Maine, is home to just over eight million people. The Austrian people are of German descent, and ninety-eight percent of them speak the German language.

In March of 1938, Adolf Hitler and the German Nazis seized Austria and deposed the Austrian chancellor, Kurt Edler von Schuschnigg. Hitler then announced the Anschluss, or union of Germany and Austria, which lasted until the end of World War II when Germany was defeated by the Allied forces.

Liechtenstein, on Austria's western border, is one of the smallest countries in the world. This tiny kingdom covers only sixty-two square miles, is less than six miles wide at the widest point from east to west, and has only about thirty-two thousand people. Like Switzerland, its neighbor to the west, Liechtenstein remained neutral throughout World War II.

Escape to Liechtenstein is a fictional account that takes place in the mountains of Austria during the late summer and fall of 1942.

CHAPTER ONE
NAZI RAID

The late afternoon shadows were slowly creeping down toward the Austrian village of Mittersill as nine-year-old Gretchen raced frantically down the steep mountainside. Her long, blond braids bounced in rhythm with her strides as her bare feet flew noiselessly through the heather. She burst through the back door of the little bungalow, her heart pounding with fear. "Hans!" she screamed. "Hans! Nazi soldiers are coming!"

Gretchen's tall, blond brother rushed into the tiny kitchen, his handsome face clouded with worry. "Are you sure, Gretchen?"

"*Ja,* I saw them," she gasped, struggling to catch her breath. "They're coming up the trail. Dozens of them!"

Hans took one glance at her ashen face and ran to the front room. Cautiously he opened one shutter. Gretchen was right. A whole platoon of armed men dressed in the hated green uniforms was goose-stepping up the narrow lane. The first column was already close enough for the boy to see the dreaded black swastika on the sleeve of each man's uniform.

"Oh, Hans, what will we do?" Gretchen wailed, gripping his arm so tightly that her fingernails dug painfully into his bare flesh. "What will we do?"

Hans carefully pried her fingers loose and then quickly closed the shutter. "Stay quiet," he ordered, "and stay calm. Maybe they won't come here." He secured the shutter as he spoke, then stepped across the room and bolted the heavy front door. His sister was right on his heels as he hurried into the kitchen to lock the back door and returned to the front room.

ESCAPE TO LIECHTENSTEIN

Anxiously, the two young people peered through the crack at the bottom of the shutters. Just as they had feared, the German troops were fanning out through the little village, conducting a house-to-house search. Hans could see two grenadiers standing on the tiny porch of the little cottage across the street, while others strode purposefully toward the upper streets of the sleepy little village. While they watched, the door across the street opened, and white-haired Mrs. Van Doer stepped out and greeted the soldiers pleasantly. Gretchen stifled a scream as one of the men suddenly raised his rifle in front of him and then thrust the weapon viciously at the old woman, shoving her backwards through the door.

"I wish Papa was here," the girl whispered softly, "and Mama . . ." Her voice trailed off.

Her brother nodded, wrapping one long arm around her thin shoulders and drawing her close to him. "Don't be afraid, Gretchen," he whispered gently. "God is still watching over us."

She suddenly twisted free of his embrace and spun around to face him. "How can you say that?" she demanded. "Where was God during the blitzkrieg, when the Luftwaffe bombed the French, and the panzer units attacked the villages? And where was God when the Nazi devils killed our Jewish neighbors? Where was He when they stole our automobiles and our cattle? Where was God? Could He not protect Austria from Anschluss?"

She paused for breath. Hans reached tenderly toward her, but she drew back. "Gretchen, please," he said, but she cut him off.

"Papa can't be with us, because he was forced into the army of the—the glorious Third Reich!" She spat out the words distastefully. Her voice rose to a shrill scream. "And now Mama—" She began to sob. "Mama's dead, Hans! Dead! Killed by the Nazis!"

Gretchen covered her face with her hands, then peered at him from between her fingers. "It's only been two months since that horrible day when the Stutka planes strafed our village! Have you forgotten already?" Sobbing, she allowed herself to fall against his shoulder. Tenderly, he again placed an arm around her.

The silence of the moment was shattered by the thud of a Nazi rifle butt against the front door. The room seemed to explode with the violence of the sound. The sturdy oak door, solid as it was, shook with the force of the blows.

"Open up!" a gruff German voice demanded, and the door shook under another barrage of blows from the man's weapon. "Open the door!"

"Hans, what shall we do?" Gretchen whispered.

Her brother held a finger to his lips. "Stay quiet," he whispered. "Maybe they'll go away."

But the heavy blows were repeated. "Open up!" the voice demanded again—impatient, threatening. "We know you're in there! Open up! Do we have to break down the door?"

Glancing apologetically at his sister, Hans shrugged and rose to his feet to open the door. "We're coming!" he called. "Just a moment."

As the boy lifted the bolt, the door was flung open with such force that he was slammed against the wall. Two burly soldiers leaped into the room to confront the terrified young people. One man pinned Hans against the wall with the stock of his rifle, while the other trained his weapon on the cowering Gretchen.

"Who's here with you?" the soldier asked the trembling girl.

Hans started to answer. "Just us," he said, but the Nazi standing before him rammed the rifle hard against his chest, cutting off the words.

"He wasn't talking to you, *knabe!*" the soldier snarled. "Answer only when you're spoken to!"

The first Nazi turned back to face Gretchen. "Who's in the house with you?" he asked again.

The girl was trembling so violently that she could hardly answer. She sucked in her breath in a sobbing little gasp, then stammered, "J-Just H-Hans and m-me. Th-That's all."

"Where are your mother and father?"

"M-Mama's not h-here with us r-right n-now, and P-Papa's in the army of the Th-Third R-Reich."

Hans took a deep breath as the soldier relaxed the painful pressure against his chest. "We're looking for a young boy," the man said harshly. "Have you seen any strangers in the village?"

Hans shook his head. "*Nein.*"

"Do you know what happens to traitors who shelter such criminals?"

The boy nodded. "*Ja.* But there is no one else here."

"We'll see for ourselves."

The grenadiers forced Hans and Gretchen to sit side by side on the kitchen floor; then they began to search the house. They methodically ransacked all three rooms, opening bureau drawers and spilling the contents across the floor, searching in areas too tiny to hide even a cat. It was as though they were deliberately creating as much chaos as possible.

Hans reached out and placed a gentle hand on Gretchen's shoulder, studying her face as he did. He hurt inside to see the terror written on her thin features, and he prayed silently for her. He and his sister had always been close. When they were very young, it was Hans who had watched after Gretchen during the long, dreary days when Mama had worked beside Papa in the steep fields. It was usually Hans that Gretchen turned to whenever she was troubled with a problem too large to handle by herself. He sighed. How would he take care of her now?

Sensing his gaze upon her, Gretchen turned to her brother and managed a weak smile. "I'm glad you're here with me."

Hans nodded. "We're in this together," he replied. "And remember, the Lord is watching over us."

She leaned her head against his muscular shoulder. "You always stay so calm," she observed. "You make it seem so easy to trust the Lord. But I have such a hard time trusting Him like you do. I'm afraid, Hans."

He squeezed her hand.

Finally, the grenadiers returned to the room where the young people waited anxiously. The taller soldier pointed out the kitchen door. "What's in the barn?"

"Nothing. One old cow that your troops didn't take."

"Come with us."

Hans and Gretchen stood in the doorway of the ancient barn, watching silently as one of the soldiers searched the building from top to bottom. The man even went into Olga's stall, shoved the gentle cow to one side, and dug in the manure on the floor with his bayonet.

The second soldier stood beside them, carefully watching their faces for any change of expression that would indicate that his comrade was close to unearthing any secrets. But of course, the barn was empty, and the search was fruitless.

Finally, the Nazi soldiers stomped from the barn. "Be watching for the boy," they told Hans and Gretchen. "He's an enemy of the Third Reich. Notify your section commander if you see any strangers. Heil, Hitler!" With a crisp salute and a click of their boots, they were gone.

ESCAPE TO LIECHTENSTEIN

Hans and Gretchen stood side by side in the doorway of the barn, watching the soldiers disappear down the path. An overwhelming weight of paralyzing fear settled upon them. They both realized that they had not seen the last of the dreaded Nazis. The grenadiers would return to search again.

CHAPTER TWO
THE FUGITIVE

Gretchen sank weakly to the ground. "Oh, Hans," she sobbed, "I was so frightened. I wish Papa was here."

Hans dropped to the grass and held her close until the trembling stopped. From their position above the house they could look across much of their beloved Mittersill, perched like a mountain goat on the slopes of rugged Mount Grossglockner. They watched in silence as green-uniformed men still strutted about in the winding, switchback streets below.

The sun was dropping quickly toward the hills behind the barn, and the air was growing cool as the troops goose-stepped back down the narrow mountain track that led from the village. Moments later, the roar of truck motors echoed across the quiet valley as the drivers downshifted to negotiate the hairpin turns below the village, their big green vehicles heavily laden with the Nazi troops. Hans let out a long sigh as the last of the Nazis disappeared from view.

He spoke softly. "So much hatred," he said. "An entire platoon of Nazi soldiers, just to search for one young boy. And if they had found him . . ." His voice trailed off.

"Well, I hate them, too!" Gretchen whispered as her brother had done. The horror of the sudden Nazi visit had left her fearful, yet trembling with rage. She clenched her small fists. "If it wasn't for the Nazis, Mama would still be alive!"

"Mama's with the Lord Jesus," Hans softly reminded her.

"*Ja*," Gretchen whispered, "but I wish she was here with us. I hate the Nazis!"

"But, Gretchen, it is wrong to hate."

The girl lifted her chin defiantly. "I don't care! They killed Mama!"

Hans sighed. "When we hate, we become like them."

His sister drew her knees up to her chin, then rested her cheek against her arm. She was silent as she pondered Hans's statement. The idea troubled her.

Hans suddenly held up one hand. "Sh-h! Listen!" Inside the barn, a board creaked. And then, another. Someone was walking in the loft!

Hans rolled over on his belly and snake-crawled to the side of the barn. He placed his face against the faded gray boards, trying to peer through the cracks. Gretchen joined him. While they watched, a head peeked over the edge of the loft, then a small figure in dark clothing slowly backed down the ladder. Holding a finger to his lips to warn Gretchen to silence, Hans crept into the barn.

The intruder backed right into Hans's arms. He gave a low cry of alarm, then attempted to scramble back up the ladder. Hans grabbed him by the ankles. "Do not be afraid," he called softly. "You're among friends."

Gretchen hurried into the barn as the boy climbed down from the ladder. When he turned around, she and Hans saw huge brown eyes filled with fear. The thin face was framed by dark hair and thick, dark eyebrows. The boy seemed older but was shorter than Gretchen was.

Hans relaxed his grip. "You're among friends," he said again. "Everything is all right."

"I must hide!" The boy spoke for the first time, and his voice was high-pitched, almost like a girl's. He tensed, and Hans sensed the fear that the boy was experiencing.

"We're friends," he repeated. "I'm Hans Kaltenbrunner and this is my sister, Gretchen."

The boy smiled cautiously, his eyes darting anxiously to the open barn door, then back to them. "My name is Jacob Reickhoff," he said. "I'm the reason the grenadiers came to your village."

"Why were they searching for you?" Gretchen asked.

Again Jacob glanced nervously toward the door. "We really can't talk here!"

"Come down to the house then," Gretchen suggested, but the visitor shrank from the idea.

"*Nein!* Not in broad daylight," he protested.

Hans closed the barn doors and then began to climb the ladder to the loft. "How about up here?" he asked. "You can find a quick hiding place if anyone comes near the barn."

Jacob nodded his agreement and followed them up the narrow wooden ladder. Hans stepped across the mounds of sweet-smelling hay to the window of the loft, opening it just a few centimeters. He sat sideways on a massive beam just below the window. "I can watch from here," he said.

Crouching low, Jacob crept to the window, slowly raised up just long enough for one cautious peek, and sank down on the hay. He drew a deep breath and then turned to face Hans and Gretchen. He was still trembling. He searched their faces for a long moment as though trying to decide if he could trust them. Finally, he spoke.

"I am endangering your lives by asking you this," he said slowly, "but can you help me? A storm is coming, and I would like to spend the night in your barn." He grinned suddenly. "I was planning to stay without asking, but you caught me."

Hans nodded immediately. "*Ja.* You may stay."

The boy shook his head. "Don't answer too quickly," he said. "Think about it first. There is much danger. If they find me here, they will kill me. I bring that danger upon you. If they find me here, you will die also."

Hans nodded again. "We understand that. You may stay."

Jacob looked up at him. "Can your father be trusted? Perhaps I should talk to him—"

Gretchen spoke up. "Papa is not here, and Mama is dead. The Nazis killed her."

A shadow of sympathy crossed the boy's face. "I am sorry." He looked back to Hans. "I will leave in the morning before sunrise, and perhaps I take the danger with me."

Hans gazed silently out the window. "We are not afraid to help," he assured Jacob. "The danger is everywhere. As long as the Nazis occupy Austria no one is safe—not even the sympathizers."

The young visitor suddenly laid a hand on Hans's arm. "I should not ask for this," he said, "but would you, could you, spare a small amount of food? I have not eaten in two days."

Hans and Gretchen glanced at each other, then turned and answered at the same instant, "*Ja,* of course!" They laughed, then Hans said, "We do not have much, but what we have we are willing to share. We will bring it right up to you."

"*Nein!*" The word was uttered with such force that Gretchen jumped. "You must wait until after dark! If someone sees you bringing food to the barn—"

"I will bring a milk pail, as if I were going to milk Olga," Hans suggested. "The food will be in the bottom of the pail."

Jacob frowned. "It is still risky," he said. "If a neighbor should drop by and see the food—"

Hans stood up. "It is nearly dark now, but we will wait a little while longer. I will hide the food in my clothes when I come." He and Gretchen headed across the loft, and Jacob disappeared behind a mound of hay.

Thirty minutes later, Hans and Gretchen sat in the loft watching Jacob devour boiled potatoes, thick slices of *ankerbrot,* and slabs of yellow cheese. The boy paused to take a long drink of water from the flask they offered, then wiped his mouth on the back of his sleeve. "Danke schön," he said, "and I am sorry for the danger I have placed you in." He bit hungrily into the second slice of *ankerbrot.*

Gretchen reached into her pocket, and with a proud smile, produced a treasure—a shiny red apple. "Here," she said, offering the fruit to Jacob. "We were saving it."

The boy eyed it hungrily. "Are there any more?"

Gretchen shook her head. "*Nein.* It is the only one. We want you to have it."

Jacob drew back. "*Nein,* my pretty friend. I could not take your last apple." But Hans and Gretchen both insisted, and at last, he accepted the gift.

Gretchen studied him in the dim light. "How old are you, Jacob?"

He looked up. "I am thirteen. I celebrated my bar mitz—" He stopped abruptly, fearfully, but the others didn't notice.

"Thirteen!" the girl echoed. "I am only nine, and I am as tall as you! Hans is twelve, but he is a full head taller than you!"

Jacob just nodded.

"Why are the Nazis so interested in you?" Hans asked bluntly. "They do not usually concern themselves with children. What have you done?"

Jacob leaned forward. "I must leave tomorrow," he said. "If the Nazis find me, they will kill me. I must escape across the border to Liechtenstein, and find Major Von Bronne. He will take me to my father and to safety in Switzerland."

Hans gave a low whistle. "Liechtenstein! That's over two hundred kilometers away!"

Jacob nodded. "*Ja,* but I will do it!" he declared. "I must!"

"Would it not be easier to head south, into Italy?" Hans suggested. "It's closer."

The other boy shook his head. "*Nein,*" he said, "Italy would be no safer than Austria. But Liechtenstein and Switzerland are neutral. I must make it to Liechtenstein."

"We can help," Gretchen suddenly volunteered. "We will go with you. We will help hide you from the Nazis!"

The boy shook his head sadly. "That would be kind," he replied. "But it would not be good. You do not understand the danger I would bring upon you."

Hans found himself warming to Gretchen's idea. "If you have to stay out of sight," he told Jacob, "then you do not dare ask for food or lodging. You need us! If we were to go with you, we could help you."

But Jacob shook his head. "You do not know what you are saying," he answered. He studied their faces for a long moment, struggling with a decision. "You do not realize the danger you would face. If the Nazis found us, they would kill us all." He paused. "I am a Jew."

CHAPTER THREE
PAPA'S SPYGLASS

A flaming red sun was just beginning to peek over the tops of the trees on the eastern slopes above Salzach Valley. Hans and Gretchen slipped from the house and quietly made their way to the barn. The air was crisp and cool. Wisps of fog still hung in the valley below Mittersill like a shroud. The morning sunlight sparkled on tiny drops of dew, reflecting every color of the rainbow. For one magical moment, the yard glistened and sparkled as though it were littered with a million jewels.

Gretchen carried a steaming bowl of *gulyassuppe,* which she attempted to conceal beneath her tattered black shawl. Her brother carried two potatoes and a single slice of *ankerbrot* in the bottom of the milk pail. Olga would provide milk for the simple meal.

Hans and Gretchen had stayed up late discussing their role in the Jewish fugitive's escape to the safety of the Liechtenstein border and had finally reached a decision. They would accompany Jacob on the treacherous journey. If Jacob agreed, the day would be spent in preparations for the trip, and they would leave shortly before sunrise the next morning.

Hans swung the barn door halfway open. "Jacob," he called softly, "It's us." But there was no answer. "Jacob," he called again, "It's us. Hans and Gretchen." But the barn was quiet and empty.

"Hans, he's not here!" Gretchen cried in alarm.

"Gretchen! Not so loud!" Her brother quickly searched the cattle stalls, Olga's and the three empty ones, peered into the granary in the corner, then scurried up to the loft. Gretchen followed him up the ladder. But the loft, too, was empty.

Hans plopped backwards into the hay and let out a long sigh. "He's gone," he said in disappointment. "He left without telling us."

"And we were going to help him," Gretchen said softly.

Hans nodded. "But I don't think he realized just how much he needs our help. Being a Jew, his life is in danger every step he takes. We could have eliminated some of the risk for him. But perhaps he really didn't trust us."

But at that moment, the ladder creaked gently, and Jacob's smiling face appeared at the edge of the loft. "*Guten morgen,* Hans. *Guten morgen,* Gretchen."

"Jacob!" Gretchen cried in delight. "We thought you were gone!" She raced across the hay and threw her arms around the startled Jewish boy.

Jacob held a finger to his lips to remind her of the need for subdued voices. "I had to take precautions," he replied.

"But where were you?" Hans puzzled. "We searched the entire barn!"

Jacob smiled modestly. "When you have been a fugitive for as long as I, you learn to make yourself invisible when the need arises. This barn has many good hiding places that you do not know about."

Gretchen offered him the steaming bowl that she carried. "Here, eat this while it's still hot," she coaxed. Hans descended the ladder and milked Olga, returning with a dipperful of the creamy white milk for Jacob.

"We have decided," he told Jacob as the boy finished his meal. "We are going with you."

The Jewish boy shook his head. "*Nein,* it is too risky. I must go alone."

"As a Jew, you will never make it to the border without us," Hans argued. "You need us."

Jacob shook his head emphatically. "I would put you in too much danger. I must go alone."

"You'll never make it by yourself! You dare not ask for food or directions! If we travel with you, we can reduce the risks."

"You do not know the risks you would be taking for me," Jacob replied. "I cannot allow that."

Hans glanced at Gretchen and then back to Jacob. "Gretchen and I are aware of the risks," he said quietly, "and we're willing to take them. We are coming with you!"

Jacob shrugged, and Hans could see that he was relenting. "You honor me by risking your lives for mine," he said softly, "but are you sure you know the dangers involved?"

The brother and sister nodded. "We discussed it last night."

Jacob sighed. "*Danke.*"

Hans stood up. "We should leave tomorrow just before sunrise. There is much to do today in preparation. We must gather supplies for the journey, and I must make arrangements for a trusted neighbor to tend to Olga, our three hens, and our garden."

Hans pulled a flask of water from his jacket and handed it to his new friend. "Gretchen and I will return at nightfall with news of our preparations and another meal," he said.

Jacob nodded and then solemnly shook hands with both of them. "Until tonight," he said. "Use caution."

The huge pot bubbled merrily on the cast iron cook stove. "I'm cooking the rest of the potatoes," Hans told Gretchen. "We'll carry them with us in the morning."

ESCAPE TO LIECHTENSTEIN

Gretchen nodded, glancing up briefly from her packing. She hefted the bulging rucksack. "This is getting heavy," she observed. "If we put too much more in, we won't be able to carry it."

Hans stepped up behind her and playfully pulled one of her braids. "Take only what is necessary," he cautioned. "This will be a long journey, and we are walking every kilometer of the way."

"Do you think we should take this?" the girl asked, holding up an old brass telescope.

Hans shook his head. "Papa's spyglass won't do us much good," he chided. "What would we use it for?"

"We could use it to watch for Nazis," his sister replied, extending the three tubular sections to their full length and peering through the instrument at the hill behind the barn. The sun was setting, and the long evening shadows gave her a strange uneasy feeling when she viewed them through the glass. She focused on the rugged cliffs of Shepherd's Pass, a jagged gap between the mountain peaks above the village. The pass was nearly a kilometer away, but the magic of the glass brought the details so close it gave her the feeling of being able to reach out and touch the rocks. Suddenly, she gave a little cry. "Hans! The Nazis are returning!"

He glanced at her. "Don't be a donkey," he snorted. "What would they be doing up there?"

With trembling hands she offered him the spyglass. "See for yourself," she said quietly. "I saw two of them."

Hans focused the glass and studied the mountainside. "I don't see anything," he reported. "Your eyes are playing tricks on you."

"I saw them," she insisted. "They were traversing the ravine just below the crest of the pass, and they both had rifles. I saw them."

Her brother swung the glass slowly from side to side. "Well, they're not there now," he said with a laugh, still peering through the instrument. "The mountainside is just as bare and empty as—" The words died in his throat. His hands trembled as he studied the rugged incline. He lowered the spyglass slowly. "You were right," he told Gretchen. "I just saw four of them, and it's obvious that they're heading for the village."

"Why would they come that way?" his sister asked. "It would take all day to climb the pass from the other side. Why didn't they just come up the road?"

Hans closed the telescope with a snap. "They wanted the element of surprise," he said. "And I know right where they're heading!" He thrust the telescope into the rucksack and quickly tied the straps.

"Gretchen," he said, "they're coming here to search for Jacob. They'll be here any minute. We have to leave now!" He thrust the loaded rucksack into her hands. "Carry this to the barn quickly," he told her. "Every second counts!"

CHAPTER FOUR
HIDING PLACE

Hans, Jacob, and Gretchen lay on their bellies in a thicket at the top of the ridge, concealed from view by the dense foliage about them. Hans held the spyglass to his eye, quietly studying the barn and house below. "Thirteen of them," he reported to the others. "Eight are searching the barn, and I counted five going into the house. We got out just in time."

He sat up and handed the spyglass to Jacob, then suddenly clapped a hand to his forehead. "The fire!" he exclaimed. "It was still burning in the cook stove. If they have any intelligence at all, they will know that we left hurriedly and cannot be far away. They will track us!"

Hans whipped open the rucksack, grabbed the first item of clothing he came to—a heavy blue shirt—and spread it out on the grass. He slid the pot of potatoes over beside the shirt and began to pile the half-cooked potatoes on the shirt.

His sister was alarmed. "Hans," she scolded, "that's your only spare shirt."

He shrugged. "Food for the journey is more important than clothing right now," he reasoned, "and a few wrinkles won't matter anyway." He tied the cloth closed to form a sack and then handed it to Jacob.

With the rucksack hanging securely from its straps across his shoulders, Hans crept backwards into the thicket, dragging the pot with him. "Hurry!" he whispered to the others. "They'll be coming after us soon." When they were on the back side of the thicket, sheltered from view of the house, he stood to his feet and hurled the pot as far as he could into the woods.

The three young people hurried along the crest of the ridge, thankful for the thick groves of boxwood and chestnut that partially concealed them from the village below. Their hearts pounded furiously. Their escape from the Nazis had been too close. All three realized that they were still in extreme danger. They half ran, half slid down the steep slope until they reached the comparative safety of the valley.

A wide, shallow stream tumbled and gurgled as it splashed along its rocky bed. Gretchen sank gratefully in the lush grass beside the crystal clear water.

But Jacob immediately grabbed her hand and pulled her to her feet. "*Nein!* There is no time to rest!" he said urgently. "They are not far behind us. We must go on!"

As if to back up his statement, at that moment a voice echoed through the woods, barking orders in German. The soldiers were indeed on their trail. Jacob waded into the stream, beckoning for the others to follow. "We must wade in the brook for a kilometer or two," he said. "It will make our trail harder to follow."

They splashed into the stream. The water came only to the middle of their shins, but the current was swift and threatened to sweep them off their feet. "Be careful," Hans called softly. "We do not want to spend the night in the woods in wet clothing."

Ten minutes later, Jacob suddenly stopped. "Wait here," he instructed the others. "I will be right back." While they watched, he dashed up the bank, ran into the woods a short distance, then dashed back into the water. As they resumed their hurried march down the creek bed, he called over his shoulder, "If they put the dogs on our trail, that will give them a false trail to follow." In the next ten minutes, he repeated the performance three more times.

After a time, they came to a huge outcropping of granite that rose above the edge of the bank. Jacob pointed to it. "We'll get out there," he said. He pointed up the slope where the rocky ridge disappeared into the forest. "Our tracks on the rocks will dry in five minutes," he explained, "so this is the ideal place to leave the water. If we stay in the stream much longer, they'll catch up to us."

Fifteen minutes later, they paused momentarily to rest atop a cliff that jutted out over the canyon. Crouching at the base of a pine tree which offered them some concealment, they studied the valley below. As they watched, a dozen soldiers in the familiar green uniforms suddenly burst out of the trees, following the course of the stream. The trio on top of the ridge quietly melted back into the woods.

Jacob shook his head in disappointment. "They're on our track, all right," he said sadly. "I was hoping it would take them longer than this to unravel our trail."

"Let's get going," Hans urged.

The other boy shook his head. "Rest a moment longer," he suggested. "At this point, I'd say we have about a twenty-minute lead on them. I need to watch and see if they pick up our trail where we left the stream." He pushed his way back through the trees. Hans and Gretchen waited impatiently, fear nagging at their minds.

Hans squeezed Gretchen's hand tenderly. "Are you all right, Gretchen?"

She looked up at him and nodded. "But I'm afraid, Hans!"

He squeezed her hand again. "This is scary, isn't it?" he replied. "But we're in this together! We'll have to trust God to take care of us." As he gazed down into her worried face, his heart went out to her. *Dear God,* he prayed silently, *help me to take care of Gretchen!*

The Jewish boy was back shortly. "They missed the point where we left the stream," he reported happily, "and they continued on down stream. That will buy us a little more time." He reached for the pack on Hans's back. "My turn to carry this for a while."

He glanced at the sky, noting with satisfaction that the daylight was fading rapidly. "Well, they won't catch us tonight," he said with relief. "Once it's dark, we'll be able to travel much faster than they can follow. It's mighty hard to read trail at night."

Jacob paused and pulled a small compass from a pocket, then studied its face in the dying light. "We need to head southwest," he told Hans. "The town of Unterkrimml is only thirty kilometers from here. I figure we can make it in two days, rugged country or no. But we need to travel all night and put as many kilometers as possible between us and the grenadiers."

He tucked the compass back into his pocket. "We will have a full moon," he said. "That will make the going easier for us, but it will also make us that much easier to spot."

He turned to Gretchen. "Think you can hike for a while longer?" he asked. "We have to go on." She nodded wearily.

ESCAPE TO LIECHTENSTEIN

Late in the afternoon of the third day, the exhausted young people crouched in a thicket on a hillside overlooking the peaceful little town of Unterkrimml. Two young men in simple clothing chatted in animated conversation as they led a slow, lumbering ox along a narrow lane flanked on both sides by low stone walls. A large, cinnamon-colored dog trotted passively beside one of the men. Blue-gray columns of smoke rose from several chimneys, meeting high in the air to form a lazy cloud over the rooftops. The voices of unseen children at play drifted up from the streets.

Gretchen sighed deeply, relieved that, at last, they had reached Unterkrimml. The last two days had been extremely difficult. Driven by the knowledge that capture by the Nazi troops meant certain death and perhaps torture, Gretchen, Hans, and Jacob had traveled hard, stopping only occasionally for brief rest periods. In forty-six hours, they had covered over thirty kilometers through the Austrian Alps, some of the most rugged terrain in all of Europe. They had seen no sign of pursuit since that first terrifying evening, and Jacob had finally agreed it was time for a rest.

"We're out of food completely," Hans said, as they silently surveyed the little village below. Jacob just nodded.

"I'm tired of half-cooked potatoes, anyway," Gretchen complained. "I'm glad they're gone!"

"You should be thankful we had them," her brother replied. "It was potatoes or nothing."

Jacob studied the town. "It would be good to have food and lodging tonight," he said. "But we do not know who we can trust. Nazi sympathizers in this country are too numerous to count. We must be careful."

He looked at his two friends. "Why don't you two head into the village?" he suggested. "If you see a likely-looking place, stop and ask. I will remain hidden on the hill unless you come for me."

He took the rucksack from Hans. "It is better to be safe than sorry," he said. "If there is any doubt, do not come for me. I will spend the night in the forest. Use caution."

A heavyset woman in a dress that had seen better days was weeding a tiny garden at the side of a small, white house on the upper side of the road. She looked up and smiled at Gretchen and Hans as they walked by, and they saw a kind, motherly face beneath her floppy, blue bonnet. They paused in the road, and she straightened up from her work and ambled toward them. Hans approached the stone wall that bordered her property, and Gretchen followed.

"*Guten tag,*" the woman said, laying a calloused hand on top of the wall as though she were settling in for a neighborly chat. "I haven't laid eyes on you before, have I?"

Hans shook his head. "*Nein, Frau,*" he said politely. "We're not from around here. We're just passing through."

"Where are you heading?" she asked, then laughed when they hesitated. "Oh, well," she chuckled, "I'll ask you no questions, and you'll tell me no lies. *Ja?*"

"We're looking for a place to spend the night," Gretchen volunteered, and the woman's eyes twinkled as she laughed again at the girl's forthrightness. Her voice had a merry, cheerful quality to it, and both young people were immediately attracted to her.

"Come right in," she invited, swinging the little wooden gate open and moving her heavy bulk to one side to allow them to pass. "I don't have much, but I can always add a little water to the soup." She closed the gate behind them.

"Perhaps we can help with some chores," Hans said as he and Gretchen stepped up onto the little porch. "Does your cow need to be milked?"

ESCAPE TO LIECHTENSTEIN

The woman waddled up the wooden steps, then wiped the perspiration from her brow as she turned to face him. "The Nazi devils got my cow," she answered. "Took her over a year ago. I've been saving and praying for another ever since." A faraway look came into her eyes, "Someday, somehow, I'll have another."

As the woman sliced carrots at her kitchen table, Hans sat across from her, studying her face. Finally, he took a deep breath and ventured, "We have a friend with us."

The big woman nodded knowingly. "*Ja,* the Jewish boy," she said, her eyes twinkling.

Hans sprang to his feet in alarm. "How did you know?" he cried.

Their hostess chuckled and motioned him back to his seat. "Relax, young man," she coaxed. "Your secret is safe here."

As he slumped back into his seat she explained, "The Gestapo was here this morning looking for you. They searched every house, and they asked a lot of questions. It was frightening. They did not tell us that they were looking for Jewish fugitives, but I put two and two together. You two obviously are not Jewish, so your friend must be."

She motioned toward the back door. "Bring him in the back way. It's safer. And if he is as hungry as you two, he'll be mighty anxious to put his feet under my table."

Half an hour later, as the three, hungry young people gratefully finished a meal of *gulasch* and *simonbrot,* their generous hostess leaned forward. "You do know that the Gestapo is searching for you," she began. "You are safe for the night, but I would advise leaving before daybreak."

She pursed her lips and looked from one anxious face to another. "May I make a suggestion? We need to get you out of those clothes. I have a huge trunk full of old things in the cellar, and I know there will be something that will fit each of you. A small detail, perhaps, but it could save your lives."

She stood and lit a thick, white candle, then handed it to Hans. "The trunk is down here," she said, throwing open a door to reveal a narrow flight of stairs. "Bring it up into the kitchen where we can see better. It is heavy, and it will take all three of you to carry it."

Holding the candle high, Hans led Jacob and Gretchen down into the cellar. A huge trunk sat alone in one corner. As Hans set the candle down, the door at the top of the stairs suddenly slammed shut, and all three heard the ominous sound of a heavy bolt being thrown.

Hans dashed up the stairs and threw his weight against the unyielding door. "Wait!" he cried. "What are you doing?"

The woman's muffled answer through the heavy door brought a chill of horror to the captives. "The Nazis are offering a reward for your capture," she said. "I will have my cow!"

CHAPTER FIVE
PRISONERS!

Gretchen ran to the top of the stairs and beat her fists against the heavy door. "You let us out!" she screamed furiously. "You're nothing but a dirty, lying Nazi!"

"Gretchen, Gretchen," Hans said, shaking his head. "That's not the way!" He took her by the shoulders and led her gently down the stairs. He sat on one corner of the trunk, and she collapsed in a heap against him. Jacob shuffled over and awkwardly sat beside them.

"I-I'm sorry," Jacob stammered. "As I feared, I have gotten you into extreme danger. It is my fault."

Hans shook his head. "*Nein,*" he said, "we're all in this to-gether. But the Lord can get us out." Jacob gave him a strange look.

Hans gazed about, studying the dim little room that held them captive. The candle had flickered out, but a small amount of light came through one small window above them. He could see that the room was bare except for the trunk they were now sitting on. An idea suddenly came to him, and he sprang to his feet.

"We can escape through the window," he whispered tri-umphantly to the others.

"*Nein,* it's too high," Gretchen objected. "We can't reach it."

"*Ja,* we can," her brother assured her. "We can stand on top of this trunk and give each other a boost." He turned to Jacob. "Help me move it under the window."

The boys tugged at the sturdy iron handles at each end of the trunk, but it refused to budge. Gretchen came over and pushed while they pulled, but still with no results. "Incredible!" Jacob puffed. "It doesn't look that heavy."

"Let's all three work on one end at a time," Hans suggested. "Jacob, let's you and I grab this handle with both hands and see if we can swing this end around together. Gretchen, you push while we lift."

They strained until their faces were red from the effort, but the trunk didn't move. Finally, they flopped on top of it for a breather. "It's fastened to the floor," Hans finally realized. "Ten men couldn't move it!"

Gretchen burst into tears. "What are we going to do? When the frau comes back with the Nazis, they're going to kill Jacob! And maybe us too!"

Hans looked from Jacob to Gretchen. "There's only one thing we can do now," he said softly. "We need to pray." He turned back to Jacob. "Gretchen and I are Christians," he explained.

The Jewish boy nodded. "I know," he replied. "I saw you pray when we ate. I chose not to notice it." He walked to the other side of the room, remarking over his shoulder, "Do what you wish. I will have no part in it."

The two Kaltenbrunners knelt beside the trunk. "Father, we ask in Jesus' name that You would help us right now," Hans prayed softly. "You know the terrible danger we are in, and we need Your help. Please show us what to do. Help us to escape from the Nazis. In Jesus' name, Amen."

As they stood to their feet, Jacob confronted them, his eyes flashing fire. "You blaspheme!" he accused them. "You blaspheme the holy name of God!"

Hans took a deep breath, then replied, "Jacob, we pray in the name of Jesus, as the Scriptures instruct us to."

ESCAPE TO LIECHTENSTEIN

The Jewish boy spat on the cellar floor. "Jesus Christ was a traitor! He turned his back on the commands and teachings of Moses."

"Jesus came as your Messiah," Hans replied softly, "if you will only receive Him."

Jacob advanced toward Hans, his fist raised. Hans was certain the other boy was going to strike him. The Jewish boy was so angry he was trembling. But Jacob paused, exhaled sharply through clenched teeth, and lowered his hand. He spat again on the floor. "Believe what you want," he told Hans. "It is none of my affair. But do not pray in . . . in that name ever again in my presence."

Hans sat down again on the trunk and began to pray silently for his troubled Jewish friend. *I wasn't even thinking about his soul,* he told himself ruefully. *If the Nazis do find us and kill us, Jacob will lose more than his life. His soul will be lost for all eternity.*

He looked up as Gretchen quietly sat down beside him, her teeth clenched in rage. Hatred for the woman who held them captive was written vividly across her face. *Change her heart, Lord,* Hans prayed silently. *Help her to see that hatred and bitterness will only hurt her.*

A door suddenly slammed upstairs, and the three captives paused as they heard heavy footsteps cross the porch. "She's going out to send for the Nazis," Jacob said. "We must escape while she is gone."

Hans studied the window. "Together we can lift Gretchen to the window," he suggested. "She can break out the glass with one of our boots and then crawl to freedom."

"And how do we get out?" Jacob asked. "Perhaps you could lift me, but then you are stuck here."

"You two can go for help," Hans answered.

Jacob shook his head. "There is no time," he replied. "And who do we ask? We have already found one Nazi sympathizer."

The three captives sat silently on the trunk, each fully aware of their desperate plight. *We can't expect any mercy at the hands of the German soldiers,* Hans thought to himself. *At best, they'll simply shoot us; they're certainly not known for their kindness. They could even—* He shook his head, as if to clear his thoughts. His imagination was conjuring up visions that were terrifying.

Jacob leaped to his feet. "I've got it!" he whispered exultantly. Hans and Gretchen looked at him quizzically.

Jacob ran up the stairs and stopped on the middle step. He stepped over the railing, leaned far out, and grasped an iron pipe overhead with both hands. While his friends watched in amazement, he swung hand over hand across the little room all the way to the outside wall. The pipe exited through the wall less than half a meter from the window.

When he was close to the wall, the boy swung both legs high, then kicked his boots through the window. The glass shattered. Carefully, he withdrew one leg, caught his heel on the windowsill to hold his weight, and used his other foot to kick out the triangular shards of glass remaining in the window frame. When most of the glass was gone, he swung back down to a vertical position and dropped easily to the floor.

Gretchen stared at him wide-eyed. "Did you cut yourself?" she asked.

Jacob shook his head. "*Nein,* I don't think so," he answered. "My boots protected me."

He turned to Hans. "Hurry!" he urged. "Here is our way out! We can lift Gretchen through the window, then you and I can swing across to the window, as I have just done. Can you do it?"

Hans shrugged. "I think so," he replied, "but I'm not as much of a monkey as you."

The other boy laughed. *"Gut!"* he smiled. "Then, let's make haste!" He picked up the rucksack, remarking as he did, "How did you come to bring this down with us? That is amazing!"

Hans shrugged. "I don't know," he replied. "Maybe God led me to."

Jacob wrinkled his nose in reply. He swung the heavy rucksack back and forth three times and then pitched it neatly through the broken window. Three minutes later, the three young people darted up the hill, hardly daring to believe that they were free. The sentence of death had been lifted. Gretchen had received a small cut on her knee from a tiny shard of broken glass, but they were no longer prisoners. God had answered their prayer.

They paused at the edge of the woods and studied the village below. All was quiet. Their escape had not been detected. With sighs of relief, they hurried up the slope. "We need to hurry," Hans urged, adjusting the straps on his pack. "There is no telling how soon she will return with the Nazis."

"I'm afraid we're in for another all-night trek," Jacob observed. "And we won't quite have a full moon tonight."

Gretchen laughed. "It doesn't matter," she said. "I'm so happy right now, I think I could walk for a week without stopping! God answered our prayers!"

Jacob turned on her. "Don't forget," he said through clenched teeth, "that I'm the one who figured the way out for us. God didn't do anything." Gretchen stared at him in silence.

Twenty minutes later, the trio paused atop a ridge to catch their breath. Dense woods surrounded them on all sides. Jacob pulled the compass from his pocket and unfolded a small, wrinkled sheet of paper. Gretchen and Hans crowded in close and realized that they were looking at a homemade map of Austria. Rivers, mountain ranges, villages, and towns were drawn in dark ink.

Jacob touched a finger to the paper. "We are right here," he told them. "Ten kilometers south of us is the town of Krimml. I do not think it is wise to go there."

He looked from one face to another. "We know for sure that the Nazis are searching for us. They beat us to the village. Once our lady friend sounds the alarm, Krimml will be the first place they will look."

He pointed to another town. "I personally think we should head for Hintertux. It is out of our way somewhat, but I believe we would be safer there. The problem is, it will take us a good two days to reach it. What do you suggest?"

Hans cupped his chin in his hands, studying the map. "We're with you," he finally said. "You seem to know your way around, and we'll trust your judgment. What do you say, Gretchen?"

Two evenings later, the trio emerged from the forest at the edge of a bluff overlooking the bustling little city of Hintertux. The trip had been hard. Berries, nuts, and a few edible roots that Jacob found had been their only food. The travelers were hungry, tired, and discouraged.

Jacob flopped down on the ground beside Hans. "We must have food," he said, "but we cannot afford to take any chances. Be very cautious. The Nazis may already be searching for us here."

"I don't get it," Hans replied with a frown. "Sure, you're Jewish and all that, but it almost seems like the entire German army is after us. Why are they so interested in capturing one young Jew?"

Jacob just shrugged. He crept to the edge of the precipice and sat down, dangling his feet over the edge.

Hans stood to his feet. "Perhaps it would be best if I go alone," he said. "If the Nazis are looking for us here, they are looking for three of us. Gretchen, stay here with Jacob. I'll be back shortly."

As Hans turned away, Jacob gave a sudden cry of surprise and alarm. Hans spun around in time to see the edge of the bank crumble away, taking Jacob with it. He and Gretchen watched in shock as their friend tumbled head over heels in a confusion of boulders, dirt, and small bushes.

When the landslide ground to a stop some distance down the slope, Jacob lay still, his body sprawled in the dirt like a crumpled doll. Hans called to him. "Jacob, are you all right?"

The boy feebly raised his head. "My ankle's hurt bad," he called. "I think it's broken!"

CHAPTER SIX
THE OLD MANSION

Hans stood at the top of the bluff, staring down in dismay at his injured friend. He fought desperately to still his rising panic. *If Jacob's leg is broken, there will be no way that he can travel. The Nazis will find us after all. God, help us!* He prayed silently, doing his best to remain outwardly calm for Gretchen's sake.

Gretchen's voice broke into his troubled thoughts. "Hans! We need to help Jacob! Do something!"

Hans glanced about, searching for a safe way down the bluff. Gretchen pointed. "We can get down that ravine if we're careful." Her brother nodded.

Slipping and sliding in the loose shale, they made their way gingerly down to their injured friend. Blood streamed down the side of his face. Jacob was now sitting up, holding his right ankle with both hands. "It hurts terribly!" he groaned through clenched teeth as they approached. "I think I broke it."

Hans knelt beside his friend. "Never mind the ankle right now," he said. "Let me take a look at that head injury." He gently parted Jacob's hair with his fingers, exposing a deep gash. He pulled his own shirttail out of his belt, ripped off a strip of fabric, then folded it into several thicknesses.

"Here," he said, placing the makeshift bandage over the wound. "Put some firm pressure on this to stop the bleeding. You've got a nasty gash, but I don't think it's serious. A head wound always bleeds a lot, making it look a lot worse than it really is."

Jacob held the fabric in place with the heel of his hand while Hans attempted to remove his boot. When Hans pulled on the boot, Jacob winced in pain.

"Sorry," Hans said, "but it has to come off." He gripped the boot in both hands and pulled with a steady pressure until it slipped free. He was more than a bit startled when Jacob leaned forward and snatched the boot from his grasp.

The ankle was already discolored and had started to swell. "You're not going to walk on that for a while," Hans told his friend. "I'll head into town and get help."

"Nein!" Jacob tried to stand to his feet, grunted in pain, then sank back to a sitting position. "Hans, we don't dare go into town! We made a mistake last time, trusting that woman. How do we know it will be any different this time?"

The blond boy gingerly touched the swollen ankle. "Well, you can't walk on this," he replied, "and we're out of food. We need to get help."

Jacob shook his head vehemently. "Have you already forgotten last time?"

"We made a grave mistake last time," Hans admitted. "But our mistake was not in choosing the wrong person to trust. Our mistake was forgetting to pray before we made our choice."

He glanced at Gretchen and then turned back to Jacob. "I think we ought to pray and ask God to show us the right person, then go into town trusting Him to guide us."

The injured boy disagreed. "It doesn't work that way," he protested.

But Hans stood firm. "It does for those who know Jesus Christ as their Savior," he replied softly. Jacob moaned in pain but didn't answer.

Hans motioned for Gretchen to follow him, then walked down the slope out of earshot of the Jewish boy. When his sister joined him, they knelt together in the leaves. "Father, we need You desperately," Hans prayed softly. "We need help, yet we do not know who to ask. We dare not approach the wrong house. We ask in Jesus' name that You would guide us to the right people. And, Father, work in Jacob's heart and help him to receive Jesus as his Messiah and Savior. In Jesus' name, Amen."

Gretchen slipped her hand into his as they walked back up the hill. "Hans," she whispered, "I'm afraid."

He nodded. *"Ja,"* he replied, "I am too."

She glanced up at him in surprise.

"But this is one of those times," he continued, "when we just have to trust the Lord."

Moments later, Hans hurried down the slope, then turned and waved to Jacob and Gretchen just before he crossed the ridge that hid them from view. His heart was pounding as he approached the city. What if he chose the wrong person to ask for help? "Lord, guide me," he prayed fervently as he stepped into the roadway.

He passed a section of bombed-out buildings, shaking his head as he viewed the damage. The broken buildings with their crumbling walls and missing roofs were unsettling to observe. The structures loomed over him like giant, eerie tombstones, silent reminders of the horrors of war. He hurried past them, zigzagging around the bomb craters in the street. News of the bombing raids had reached Mittersill on many occasions, and he had heard of the heavy damage inflicted on various Austrian cities, but this was the first time he had actually witnessed the results. He was deeply moved and saddened by the scene.

He glanced about fearfully, studying the face of each person he passed, hoping to avoid attracting any unwanted attention. But no one gave him a second glance.

He entered a quiet residential section. *Lord,* he prayed silently, *You have someone in one of these homes that You have chosen to help us. Guide me to that person.*

Hans glanced up to notice that he was passing a large, forbidding mansion hidden behind a high stone wall. He paused at the wrought iron gate and caught a glimpse of rose gardens and ornamental shrubbery surrounding a large, gray-blue house with white shutters. The building was showing signs of decay, and the grounds were neglected, but the boy realized that the estate belonged to someone who at some time must have had tremendous wealth. But Anschluss had changed all that.

He hurried on. This, obviously, was not the place to seek help. But as he hurried down the street, his thoughts kept returning to the old mansion. Was the Lord trying to direct him to seek help at that dismal place?

Finally, he retraced his steps. "Lord," he prayed again, "in just another moment I'll be passing right by that big house. If this is the place that You are guiding me to, help me to know it."

As he passed by the gate, Hans felt compelled to stop for another glimpse of the mysterious house behind the gray stone wall. And then, he found himself actually lifting the latch and entering the property. He quietly closed the gate behind him, feeling as he did so that he was closing off his only avenue of escape. He approached the house, his heart pounding.

On the porch, he timidly raised a hand to knock, then lowered it again. What if this was the wrong place? "Lord, help," he whispered. He raised his hand, lowered it again, then raised it a third time. Taking a deep breath, he knocked.

The door opened almost immediately, and Hans found himself staring up into the bearded face of a huge, unsmiling man. *"Ja?"* the man said, his dark eyes striking fear into the boy's heart. This was the wrong house, but it was too late!

"I-I'm looking for help," Hans stammered. His heart pounded frantically, and he suddenly felt very small and very vulnerable.

The big man took a step forward, glanced once to the right and once to the left as if to check the street, then seized Hans by the arm. He jerked the frightened boy into the house and slammed the door.

CHAPTER SEVEN
THE UNDERGROUND

Hans stared in terror at the huge stranger. The man was at least two meters in height with huge shoulders and arms that suggested strength enough to lift a horse. A thick black beard covered most of the stern face. The man studied Hans without speaking, his dark, intense eyes striking fear into the boy's heart.

Suddenly, the thick beard parted in a smile to reveal the whitest teeth Hans had ever seen. To his amazement, the man boomed, "The Lord sent you here. I know it!" He extended a huge bear paw of a hand. "I'm Lars," he said. "And what can I do for you, Brother—"

"Hans," the boy said, timidly shaking the man's hand. "Hans Kaltenbrunner. And I do need your help."

The big man shook his head. "Around here, Hans, we never mention last names. It's always safer that way."

He laughed at the puzzled look on the boy's face. "We've been involved with the Underground for two years now, and you're the first to ever volunteer a last name. You're new to this, *ja?*"

Hans stared again. *The Underground! Papa had told many fascinating stories about the network of brave people secretly helping Jews to escape to safer countries, but I had never, in all my wildest dreams, ever expected to meet any of them!* He let out his breath slowly. "Are you . . . are you a believer?" he asked timidly.

"*Ja,* I met my blessed Savior when I was a boy about your age, Hans," Lars replied. "And you're a believer too. I can tell."

He gave a hearty chuckle. "I'm sorry if I startled you when you came in the door a moment ago," he said, "but I had to get you out of sight fast. Rule number two around here: never use the street entrance."

He led Hans into a large sitting room, indicating with a sweep of his hand that the boy was to be seated. Hans sat down on a faded velvet sofa, and Lars took a seat across from him. He leaned forward.

"Hans, the Lord told me this morning that someone would come for help today," he said. "What can we do for you?"

Hans hesitated, wondering exactly how much he should tell this friendly stranger. The experience with the cunning hostess of two nights previous had taught him to be wary.

The big man sensed his reluctance to talk. He sat back and crossed his arms. "Hans," he said, "tell me only what I need to know to help you. Believe me, it's better that way for both of us. People with too much information end up getting hurt."

He grinned suddenly. "Suppose I tell you what little I know. Would that help? Let's see. There are three of you traveling together, and one of you is Jewish. You're moving as fast as possible to get out of the country, and you're heading for Liechtenstein or Switzerland. The Nazis are close on your trail. Am I right so far?"

Hans stared at him. "How did you know?"

Lars laughed. "Word gets around on the Underground, and you three are big news. The Nazis have been combing the countryside looking for you. The Gestapo is everywhere. I don't know what all is going on, but it's more than just the fact that a Jew is involved. It almost seems that half of Hitler's forces are searching for you. Something big is up."

He twisted his beard. "How can we help?"

Hans leaned forward. "We've been traveling for two days with no real food. Jacob—he's the Jewish boy—fell over a cliff this afternoon, and we think he broke his ankle. We need a doctor to look at his leg, and we need a place to stay until he gets better."

A look of concern passed across Lars's face. "I'm sorry to hear of the accident," he said. "How far did he fall?"

"Six or eight meters," Hans answered. "His ankle was swelling pretty badly when I left him."

"Who else is with you?"

"My sister, Gretchen."

"How old is she?"

"Nine."

The big man sat back with a frown of concentration on his face, unconsciously stroking his beard as he considered the situation. Hans sat uneasily, wondering if he had already told the man too much. Lars seemed genuinely concerned, and if he was a true Christian, he could be trusted. But the encounter with the woman at Unterkrimml had nearly cost them their lives, and Hans was wary.

Finally, Lars leaned forward and laid a huge hand on the boy's knee. "I'm glad the Lord sent you to us," he said. "We are going to have to be very careful, but we can help."

He pulled out a huge pocket watch and glanced at it, then tucked it back into his waistband. "It'll be dark in about two hours," he said. "It's crucial that we wait until then."

A slender, pretty woman with flaming red hair swept into the room just then, and Lars stood to his feet. "Hans," he said, "I'd like you to meet my wife, Rachel. Rachel, this is my friend Hans. The Lord sent him to us just now." He winked at the boy, then said, "Hans doesn't have a last name."

The smiling woman extended her hand, and Hans rose to his feet and shook it. "*Guten tag,* Hans," she said pleasantly. "We trust that we can be of help."

"Rachel, Hans and his friends haven't eaten a decent meal for quite some time, and I would imagine that they're quite hungry. The others won't be here for a while, but how about fixing something for Hans, just enough to hold him off until his friends get here and we can all dine together?"

Rachel nodded and headed to the back of the house.

Lars turned to Hans. "She'll have something for you in just a few minutes." He drummed his thick fingers on the arms of his chair and sat quietly staring at the floor, apparently deep in thought. Hans waited patiently.

"We don't dare go for your friends until after sunset," the man said suddenly. "Are you sure you can find the place where you left them, even in the dark?"

Hans nodded. *"Ja."*

"My wife will look at your friend's ankle. She is not a doctor, of course, but she will know what to do. And we will have a safe place for you to stay."

He smiled. "But we will deal with that later," he said. "And now, Hans, tell me—how did you come to the Lord?"

Hans shared his testimony with his new friend. The big man smiled and nodded as he finished. *"Ja,"* he said, "it is *gut* to be saved, is it not?"

His face suddenly took on a very serious look. "I pray every day that this war will soon be over," he said gravely. "The Allies are stepping up the pace somewhat, so maybe there is hope. The Americans have now taken Guadalcanal back from the Japanese. Their marines took the airfield and drove the Japanese into the jungles, and their navy is rebuilding the airfield for their own use."

Hans nodded. "When did this happen?"

Lars held up his hands. "Sometime in the last month or so. We just heard this week. But you know how slow the news travels."

The boy looked thoughtful. "Do you think the Allies will win this war?" he asked.

The big man frowned, his dark eyebrows suddenly giving his cheerful face a fierce appearance. "I pray every day that they will," he sighed. "Freedom will be a thing of the past if they do not. We must continue to pray."

Rachel came in and announced that a simple meal was ready for Hans. She led him to the kitchen, and he sat down to a plate of vegetables and *simonbrot*. He prayed, then started in eagerly. While he ate, he could hear Lars in the other room with a visitor. The two men were talking excitedly in low voices. Hans strained to hear what they were saying, but the words were muffled and indistinct.

Hans finished the meal, thanked his hostess, and went back to the sitting room. A thin, gray-haired man exited the room quickly as Hans entered, and Hans didn't get a look at his face. Lars didn't bother to introduce them.

The big man looked up as Hans entered the room. "Feel better with something in your belly?"

The boy smiled and nodded. "I'll admit that I was mighty hungry. I appreciate your kindness. Jacob and Gretchen must be starving by now."

As dusk settled over the city, Hans suddenly heard hollow footsteps somewhere down below. A door opened, and he heard Lars's wife call out a greeting. A moment later, a stocky man with short blond hair entered the room.

Lars shook hands with the man, exchanged warm words of greeting, and turned to Hans. "Hans," he said, "this is a man you can trust with your life. He will go with you, as he will be less conspicuous than I. Adolf, meet Hans; Hans, meet Adolf."

Adolf silently shook hands with Hans and turned to go, expecting the boy to follow him. Lars put a hand on the man's shoulder. "Use extreme caution," he said earnestly. "For some reason, the Nazis are very anxious to get their hands on these three. Do not take any chances."

The other man nodded, motioned for Hans to follow him, and led him from the room. Hans followed him downstairs to a dark, musty-smelling basement. Adolf opened the back door, and they slipped silently into the orchards behind the house. Hans noticed that their route was nearly hidden from view of the street.

When they were some distance from the house, the man spoke for the first time. "Hans," he said, "why don't you show me where your friends are? I'll follow you."

"I entered town at a place where there was a whole section of bombed-out buildings," the boy replied. "There was a green water tower that had taken a direct hit from a shell. If you can take me there the shortest way, I'll lead from there."

Adolf nodded. *"Gut."*

Ten minutes later, they left the roadway and headed into the woods. "We're almost there," Hans whispered. "The bluff is just ahead."

The black outline of the bluff loomed over them in the darkness. Hans followed its perimeter until he located the area where the slide had taken place. "This is it," he told his companion. "This is where Jacob fell."

He cupped his hands to his mouth and called softly, "Jacob! Gretchen! It's me, Hans!"

He stood still and listened but was surprised when there was no reply. "Gretchen!" he called again. "Jacob! It's Hans! Where are you? I brought help!"

ESCAPE TO LIECHTENSTEIN

But the dark hillside was quiet, and there was no answer to his calls. Hans peered into the darkness. His heart pounded with a growing sense of apprehension. Jacob and Gretchen were gone.

CHAPTER EIGHT
MONIQUE

Hans searched the dark forest in desperation. He called again, but the wind in the treetops threw his words back at him, mocking his futile attempts to locate his sister and Jacob. He shuffled through the trees until he spotted the dark silhouette of Adolf.

"I left them right here," he told the man. "What could have happened to them?"

Adolf slowly shook his head. "It is hard to tell, young friend," he replied quietly. "But do not be alarmed. We will find them." His words had a calming effect upon Hans.

"Let's head back to the road to get our bearings," Adolf continued. "We'll search this whole hillside if we have to."

Hans followed him back to the roadway, his mind in turmoil. *Where are Gretchen and Jacob? Have they been captured by Nazi soldiers or, perhaps, discovered by a traitorous citizen anxious for a reward?* "Dear God," he whispered softly as he stumbled along in the darkness, "please help us find them."

"Hans," a low voice called from the bushes right beside the trail. Hans jumped with fright, and then laughed in relief as his sister stepped into view. He hugged her with delight, and she led him to the spot where Jacob lay concealed by dense shrubbery. Adolf came hurrying over.

"Where were you?" Hans asked. "We couldn't find you up by the bluff. I was getting worried!"

"A German patrol came up the ridge just after you left," Jacob answered. "I thought they were going to step on us. As soon as they were gone, we moved down here where it's safer. We've been lying in this thicket for hours." He suddenly winced in pain and grabbed his ankle with both hands.

Hans introduced Adolf. "You will soon be among friends," the man assured them. "We have a safe place for you to spend the night."

"Believe it or not, God has led us right to the Underground!" Hans told Gretchen excitedly. He glanced at Jacob. "God does answer prayer. We'll have a safe place to stay, and they'll be able to look after your ankle."

The stocky man knelt beside the injured boy. "I'll carry you on my back," he said, "but we must be alert. Our chances of encountering a Nazi patrol tonight are very real." He helped Jacob to a sitting position, then, placing the boy's arms over his shoulders, stood to his feet with Jacob on his back. The boy still clutched his empty boot.

"We'll take a different route back," the man told Hans. "We will go through the woods. It will be considerably longer, but there will be less danger of being discovered."

Nearly an hour later, Lars greeted them warmly at the top of the stairs. "Come in, come in!" he boomed. "God has answered our prayers, and you have arrived safely."

Adolf backed over to the sofa and gently deposited his burden in it. Lars turned to Adolf, gripping the man's hand in a firm handshake. "*Danke schön,* Brother. I appreciate the risks you have taken tonight."

Adolf nodded and was gone.

"So you are Gretchen," Lars said. Gretchen stared in amazement as the huge man advanced toward her. She took an involuntary step backward.

The beautiful teeth flashed white in the black beard as Lars laughed. "Come, my child, do not be alarmed. My name is Lars, and I am a servant of the Lord. And I am told that you are a believer in Jesus Christ. Am I right?"

Gretchen nodded, then shyly shook the huge hand that was offered. She returned his smile.

Lars turned to Jacob. "And you are the young man that the führer's soldiers seek so fervently!" he said. "Jacob, welcome to my home. You will be safe here." He shook hands with the boy. "Tell me, have you found your Messiah?"

The Jewish boy jerked back violently, as if he had just been slapped in the face. He shook his head vehemently, and a dark look of displeasure crossed his face.

Rachel entered the room just then, and Lars introduced her to the new guests. "I'm glad you are finally here," she said with a friendly smile. "Lars and I have been praying for you ever since this morning, even before we knew who you were."

She knelt at Jacob's feet. "Let's take a quick look at that ankle," she said, "then I know you three will be ready for a hot supper."

Jacob winced in pain as the woman ran expert fingers over his injured limb, then groaned aloud when she grasped his foot and gently moved it from side to side. "I'm sorry I'm hurting you," she told him. "I'll be through in just a moment." She gently moved his foot up and down, then again from side to side. Jacob gritted his teeth.

The woman stood to her feet. "Good news!" she announced with a cheerful laugh. "I don't think it's broken. But you do have a bad sprain, and you will have to stay off it for a few days. I'll tape it for you right after supper, and we'll have you better in no time."

She looked at her husband. "We'll be ready to eat in ten minutes."

He nodded. *"Gut."* The big man turned back to his three young guests. "While my wife is getting the meal ready, I need to show you to your room." He chuckled. "If I don't show you, you'll never find it."

He gestured toward the huge stone fireplace. "Hans, crawl in there and push on the left side panel, would you?"

A puzzled frown crossed Hans's features, and the big man laughed. "Just do it. You'll see why in a moment."

Hans obligingly knelt at the edge of the hearth and pushed on the stones on the left side. He turned to Lars. "Nothing happened."

The man nodded. "Right," he said. "Now, let me show you something." He pointed a huge finger to the underside of the mantel above the fireplace. "If you feel right here, you'll discover a slight depression in the wood. It's the release for the door to a secret room. Hans, you push again on that same panel while Gretchen pushes the release lever."

Gretchen found the depression with her fingertips, then pushed with both hands. "It moved!" she exclaimed.

Lars nodded. "Hold it in. Now, Hans, push again on the panel."

To the amazement of the three young people, the stone work on the inside of the fireplace swung slowly out of sight, revealing a dark opening just over half a meter wide!

"Amazing!" Hans exclaimed in delight. "It's unbelievable! I couldn't even see the cracks!"

"The panel won't move unless the release is pressed at the same time," Lars informed them. "This will be your room for the next few days." He picked up a box of matches from the mantel, lit a squat white candle, and handed it to Hans. "You first. Gretchen and I will follow."

He turned back to Jacob. "We'll help you in after supper, when you are all ready to bed down for the night." Jacob nodded.

Hans crawled through the opening to discover a tiny room barely a meter wide. Two narrow bunks hung from one wall, one above the other, with just enough room for a person to stand beside them. There were no windows.

Hans held the candle for Gretchen and Lars, who squeezed in beside him. Gretchen stared about the tiny room. "What's this little room for?" she asked.

"It's a hiding place from the Nazis," Lars explained. "Over forty of God's chosen people have spent a night or two in here, on their way to freedom. Years ago, this big house was designed with this special hiding place in mind. You can measure the building outside, then measure the interiors of the rooms, one by one, and never realize that some space is missing. Don't ask me how it all works out, but it does. We'll have you three sleep in here during your stay with us just to be on the safe side. If the Nazis were to search the house suddenly, they'd never find you here."

He knelt and crawled back through the opening, and Gretchen and Hans followed. Lars pushed sharply against the edge of the panel, and it closed tightly with a gentle click. He pinched out the candle and returned it to the mantel.

Supper was a festive occasion. Lars and his wife sat at opposite ends of the long mahogany table, while Gretchen and Hans sat side by side on a wooden bench. Jacob sat across from them on the other bench, his injured leg propped up before him.

Hans studied the benches in bewilderment. Such elegant furnishings, and such crude wooden benches. They seemed completely out of place.

Lars noticed his interest in the benches. "They are safer than chairs," he explained. "If the Gestapo was to visit during meal-time, any of our guests that did not wish to be seen would simply exit to the hidden room. The others on the bench simply slide over to fill in the gap. No chairs need to be moved hurriedly." He glanced at his three young guests. "We will practice after dinner when Jacob's ankle has been cared for."

He bowed his head. "Let us pray," he said quietly. "Father, we thank You for sending these three young travelers to us safely today. We pray for Your continued watchcare and for wisdom to handle any situations that might arise. Guide them safely to the border. We give You thanks for this food that You have so gra-ciously provided. In Jesus' name, Amen."

Rachel lifted the cover from a dish, revealing a small, dark mound of steaming meat, and Gretchen squealed in delight. *"Tafelspitz!"* she exulted. "We haven't had *tafelspitz* since the Nazis invaded!"

Rachel looked pleased. *"Ja,"* she admitted, "it isn't easy to come by, but we thought it would be a welcome treat."

The three young people ate ravenously, thoroughly enjoying the hearty meal. Potatoes and garden peas, thick slices of *simonbrot* without butter, and glasses of cool milk were enjoyed by all. Finally, Lars pushed back from the table. "We can't eat like this all the time," he said, "but we are mighty thankful when the Lord does provide it, *ja?*"

He turned to Rachel. "Why don't you wrap Jacob's ankle?" he suggested. "I'll go through a drill with Hans and Gretchen." He stood up, picked Jacob up in his arms effortlessly, and carried him to the couch. Rachel followed them.

Lars deposited the injured boy gently on the couch and returned to his seat. "We need to drill you on retreating to your room," he told Hans and Gretchen. "If there is a knock at the door at any time, I want you to assume it is the Nazis and get to the hidden room as quickly as possible. Gretchen, you push the release, and Hans, you open the panel. Ready?"

He rapped the underside of the table with his knuckles. "Someone is at the door! Go!"

The two young people jumped from the bench and hurried to the fireplace. Lars followed, his huge pocket watch in his hand. Hans knelt at the panel, and Gretchen reached for the release.

"Stop!" Lars called suddenly. "It is no good. Look at the table. You must take your dishes with you. If the Nazis were to see the extra place settings, they would know immediately of your presence in the house. Sit down, and we will try again later."

All three returned to their places at the table, and Rachel continued to bandage Jacob's ankle. Lars looked from Gretchen to Hans. "Do you have any idea," he asked, "why the Nazis are so interested in your friend?"

"He's a Jew," Gretchen said hotly. "He hasn't hurt anybody, but they want to kill him, just because he's a Jew."

The man shook his head. "There has to be more to it than that," he declared. "They wouldn't put out this much manpower just to capture one young Jew."

"*Ja,* but they would," the girl insisted. "They hate the Jews. If I were God, I'd kill every Nazi in the whole world!"

Lars looked at her in surprise. "You sound quite serious about this."

"*Ja!*" Gretchen blurted angrily. "I am. The Nazis killed Mama, and now they're trying to kill Jacob, and maybe us. I hate them!" Suddenly, she burst into tears.

Lars laid a huge hand gently on hers. "Gretchen," he said softly, "hating the Nazis won't solve anything. It won't bring your mother back, and it won't help you or Hans or Jacob. Ask God to put the love of Jesus in your heart. He can help you love even the Nazis."

Gretchen glared at him. "Love the Nazis?" she echoed. "*Nein! Never! I will always hate them! Always!*" She jumped up from the table and ran from the room in tears.

Lars glanced at Hans. "She's quite bitter about this, isn't she?" he observed quietly.

Hans nodded. "I worry about her," he admitted. "Two months ago the Nazis caught wind of a rumor that a Resistance unit was forming in our village. The rumor was false, but they strafed us in retaliation, and Mama and three others were killed. Gretchen hasn't gotten over it. She's carrying a tremendous load of grief . . . and hatred."

The big man nodded knowingly. "We'll pray for her," he promised. "God can change her heart."

Hans leaned forward. "Pray for all three of us," he begged. "We have a very difficult journey ahead, and I wonder if we even stand a chance of making it to Liechtenstein. The Nazis are everywhere! I know that we're supposed to trust the Lord and all, but I worry about it. I try to be brave and trusting for Gretchen's sake, but sometimes it's so hard. . . ."

Lars smiled. "The Lord's promises are true any time," he replied. "Remember what David said in the Psalms? He didn't say, 'When things are going well, I will trust in thee.' *Nein.* He said, 'What time I am afraid, I will trust in thee.' God's promises are for the hard times—the times of peril and danger."

Gretchen entered the room just then, and Lars steered the conversation toward other topics. Moments later, he rapped sharply on the underside of the table. "The Gestapo is at the door!" he said, glancing at his watch. Hans and Gretchen leaped to their feet, snatched their dishes from the table, and raced to the fireplace. As Gretchen reached for the release, Hans leaned against the panel. When the panel opened, they crawled through, then pushed the panel closed. Lars glanced again at his watch.

The big man pushed the release and opened the panel with his foot. "Come on out," he called. "We'll try it again." As they stood to their feet beside him, Lars told them, "That took forty-four seconds—not bad for a first try. But we need to get the time down to thirty seconds." He paused. "Including Jacob."

Rachel had finished wrapping Jacob's ankle, and now she helped him hobble from the room. Gretchen and Hans returned to the table for another drill, arranging the dishes and tableware as they had been during the meal. Lars gave the signal, and they raced again for the secret room.

They repeated the exercise again and again. Lars finally tucked his watch back into his waistband. "Twenty-four seconds," he told them. "We're getting somewhere. Tomorrow, we'll include Jacob in the drills."

Rachel entered the room. "I'd like Gretchen and Hans to come with me," she told her husband. "There's someone I'd like them to meet." Lars nodded and motioned for the young people to follow her.

She led them to the rear of the huge house. They passed along a spacious hallway decorated with colorful tapestries and large paintings in ornate gilded frames, then entered a small library.

A slender, attractive girl was seated in a high-backed chair. Her long green dirndl was faded and patched, and blond curls peeked out from under the edge of her frayed, brightly-colored scarf. But her brown eyes sparkled with warmth and friendliness, and a mischievous grin gave her a carefree, impish look.

"Hans, Gretchen," Rachel said, "meet a friend of ours. This is Monique. Monique, meet Hans and Gretchen."

Hans bowed, his ruddy cheeks turning just a bit brighter as he did. *"Guten tag,"* he said, feeling awkward and unsure of himself. The girl was beautiful!

Gretchen gave a little curtsy. "Pleased to meet you," she said politely.

"It is good to know you," Monique said in a soft, pretty voice. "I am anxious to meet your friend—the Jewish boy."

Hans turned to Rachel. "Where is Jacob?" he asked, then paused in confusion as Rachel and Monique exchanged glances and burst into laughter.

It was Gretchen who caught on first. "Monique, you're a sham!" she cried. "Hans, it's Jacob!" Laughing, she lifted the hem of the long green skirt to reveal a taped ankle and a booted foot. Hans stared in amazement.

"I hate to say this, Jacob," he teased, once he had recovered from the initial shock, "but you make a lovely girl. You had me fooled."

"The Nazis are looking for a Jewish boy," Rachel explained, "and we think perhaps the disguise will throw them off the trail, should they catch up with you. Jacob is small, and with a few locks of blond hair sewn into the edge of his kerchief, he passes easily for a girl. It was his voice that gave us the idea."

Jacob pulled the second boot from its hiding place under the chair, and then Hans and Gretchen helped him hobble to the front of the house to introduce "Monique" to Lars. The big man looked up as they entered the room, then burst into laughter. "Rachel, it's perfect!" he cried. "Jacob, you could go anywhere in that outfit. Your own mother would never recognize you!"

The cheery little group froze as a heavy knock suddenly sounded at the front door. A look of consternation passed over Lars's face. "Quick!" he whispered urgently, "to the secret room! Rachel, help Jacob!"

CHAPTER NINE
THE *UNTEROFFIZIER*

Gretchen, Hans, and Jacob huddled in the darkness inside the little room. Hans knelt with his ear against the wall, trying to hear what was happening in the room outside. He could hear voices faintly but could make out none of the words; the secret room was nearly soundproof.

"Who is it, Hans?" Gretchen whispered.

Hans couldn't see his sister's face in the darkness, but he recognized the tremor of fear in her voice. He slipped an arm around her. "I don't know," he answered, "but don't worry. They'll never find us in here. Just wait quietly. And remember, God is with us."

Moments later, the secret panel popped open a crack, then Lars's big hand pushed it open the rest of the way. "You can come out now," he said. "It's safe."

Hans and Gretchen crawled out, and then waited for Jacob, who was a bit slower. Hans swung the panel closed and stood to his feet. "Who was it?" Jacob asked.

Lars waved his hand. "Just a passerby asking for directions," he replied. "Nothing to be concerned about." He glanced at Rachel with a thoughtful expression on his face. "Still, we must be careful. The Gestapo is very determined to find you—and they are searching everywhere."

The next few days passed slowly. The three young people grew restless, tired of being cooped up indoors. But they all realized the necessity of staying out of sight. Lars insisted that they practice drills each day, and they finally reached a time of twenty-one seconds with all three safely inside the secret room. Jacob's ankle healed rapidly, and within a week he was walking almost normally.

One morning after an early breakfast, Lars and Rachel hugged their young visitors. Adolf stood quietly waiting at the door to the stairs. Jacob was wearing the dirndl and kerchief.

"The Lord be with you, my young friends," Lars said soberly. "We will be praying. Trust God to get you to the border."

He cleared his throat, then continued, "Adolf will take you in his hay wagon as far as Milders, which is twenty-eight kilometers from here. He will put you on the road to Langenfeld, which is another fifteen kilometers. You are to stay the night with another Underground family. The man is named Peter. They live in a gray house at the edge of town, two doors down from the bakery. You'll find it easily. Simply tell Peter that Lars sent you. He will know what to do. When you leave Langenfeld in the morning, he will give you directions to your next stop."

He tugged at his beard. "Auf wiedersehen. God be with you." Rachel wiped tears from her eyes as Adolf opened the door, motioning for the three young people to follow him.

The sun was peeking over the eastern hills as they reached the edge of town. Wisps of fog still hung in the air, and Gretchen drew her jacket about her more tightly. The morning was cool.

Adolf led them to a wagon hidden in a grove of buttonwood trees. "Gretchen, you sit beside me," he instructed, climbing onto the wooden seat and gathering the reins in his calloused hands. "The boys can pile into the hay in back." Hans and Jacob scrambled up to perch atop the huge mound of hay. Adolf clucked to the two gray horses, and they were off.

"Keep a sharp eye out," the stocky man told them. "If we see anyone on the road, you lads bury yourselves in the hay. The search for you has apparently died down, but we can't afford to take any chances."

They rode along in silence for nearly two hours. The morning sun climbed higher in the sky, and the air grew warm. Gretchen removed her jacket.

Suddenly, Adolf stiffened. "Soldiers coming this way," he growled in a low voice. "Quickly, lads. Dig into the hay."

Gretchen turned her head slightly and watched as Jacob and Hans burrowed into the mound of hay. "Pull your foot in, Hans," she said in a low voice. "I can still see it." She reached behind her, grabbed a handful of hay and tossed it over to help cover a suspicious-looking spot.

The Nazi jeep skidded to a stop in front of them. Four German soldiers scrambled out, motioning for the wagon to halt. "Keep still," Adolf said softly to Gretchen. "Let me do the talking." He drew back on the reins, bringing the wagon to a stop six or eight meters from the vehicle.

"Hold it, old man!" a brash young *Unteroffizier* ordered, brandishing his bayonet-tipped rifle. He strutted past the horses and approached the side of the wagon. "Where do you think you're going?"

"Just taking a load of hay to Milders," Adolf replied calmly.

The Nazi gestured toward Gretchen with his weapon. "Who is this?" he demanded.

Adolf replied in the same calm voice. It was as if he had absolutely nothing to hide. "She is a friend," he replied. "Her name is Gretchen."

The young officer turned and barked an order to the soldiers. "Search the wagon!"

The three soldiers surrounded the wagon, fixed their bayonets to their rifles and began to stab the wicked-looking weapons carelessly into the load of hay. Gretchen turned her face away. Hans and Jacob would be discovered, if not killed or seriously wounded by the sharp bayonets.

CHAPTER TEN
PANTRY PANIC

The Nazi officer stood stiffly, chin held high, watching Adolf intently as the soldiers repeatedly bayoneted the golden mound of hay. But the stocky man sat hunched on the wagon seat, head lolled to one side, as though he were bored by the whole episode. The Nazi could not see that the man was praying fervently for God's protection of the two terrified boys concealed deep in the hay.

Finally, convinced by Adolf's casual demeanor that nothing was amiss, the officer called off his men. "Carry on," he told Adolf. He slapped the rear of one of the horses, laughing in amusement as the startled animal leaped forward against the harness. Gretchen sighed in relief as the wagon began to roll.

"That was scary," she remarked softly to Adolf, once the wagon was out of earshot of the soldiers.

Adolf nodded almost imperceptibly. "*Ja,* it was," he agreed. "But God was watching over us, I have no doubt. We just witnessed a miracle of His protection." He gazed for a moment over his shoulder; then, convinced that the Nazi jeep had continued on its way, he called to the boys, "Come out, lads! The danger is past!"

Jacob and Hans emerged from the mound, brushing bits of the prickly hay from their clothes. "That was close," Hans commented. "I thought we were dead!"

"God kept their blades from reaching you," Adolf assured him. "You are safe in His hands."

"It was hot under there," Jacob remarked, changing the subject. "I thought I was going to suffocate."

"Enjoy the fresh air while you can," Adolf laughed. "We are nearing Milders, and I think it would be wise for you two to hide as we pass through."

On the far side of town, he pulled the wagon to a stop. The boys again crawled from their hiding places in the hay, scratching and stretching. Adolf pulled a cloth-wrapped bundle from under the wagon seat and handed it to Jacob.

"Food for today's journey," he said simply. "A small gift from my wife." He reached into his pocket and pulled out a sheaf of bills and handed them to Hans. "And this is from Lars."

He pointed up the road. "At the bottom of that rise," he said, "the road forks. Go to the right. As Lars told you, Langenfeld is fifteen kilometers away." He solemnly shook hands with each of them. "God be with you. You are in our prayers. Auf wiedersehen."

He climbed back into the wagon seat.

"*Danke schön,* Herr Adolf, for your kindness," Jacob called.

Adolf nodded.

"We won't forget you," Hans said. "Thank Lars and Rachel again for us."

Adolf nodded again, then turned the wagon around in the roadway.

"Auf wiedersehen!" Gretchen called, waving as the wagon rolled back down the dusty road.

"Well, we're back to walking," Hans said, hunching his shoulders to adjust the straps on the rucksack. "Fifteen kilometers before supper time!"

Jacob stopped and removed the kerchief, bunching it up in his hand, then peeled the dirndl over his head. "I'm not wearing this all day!" he said. "I'll slip it back on when we get close to town."

They walked for an hour and a half and then paused beside a trickling stream to rest and eat the thick cheese sandwiches that Adolf's wife had prepared for them. They laughed together at the antics of a squirrel in the huge oak that shaded their picnic spot. The afternoon was warm, and all three were enjoying the brief rest. Bright red clumps of paintbrush and clusters of blue lupine added brilliant splashes of color on the hillside above them, creating a bright, cheery atmosphere.

Hans took a bite of his sandwich, then cocked his head, studying Jacob with a curious gaze. Finally, he cleared his throat and spoke. "Let me ask you something, Jacob," he said. "Why are you so touchy about your boots? While your ankle was in that bandage, you carried that one boot around like a good luck charm. And if anyone so much as touches one, you're ready to jump all over them."

Jacob regarded him with a cold stare, then shrugged, trying to appear casual as he answered, "The boots are special. They were given to me by Papa."

Hans nodded. "I can understand that," he said, "but you act like—" He stopped, suddenly intimidated by the angry look that appeared in the Jewish boy's eyes. "Oh, forget it," he muttered.

Suddenly embarrassed, he fumbled in his pocket. His fingers found the bills Adolf had given him, and he withdrew the money from his pocket. "Hey!" he exclaimed. "Look at this money Lars gave us. Ten fifty-schilling notes. He gave us five hundred schillings!" Forgetting his questions regarding Jacob's boots, he counted the money again, then stuffed it back in his pocket.

Late in the afternoon, they passed a deserted farm. The barn had been burned to the ground, and the farmhouse windows were boarded up. The property was silent and desolate. "Better change into Monique," Hans told Jacob with a grin. "I think we're approaching town."

Minutes later, the trio stood quietly in the road, studying a small gray house. Four noisy children played on the porch, and several scrawny chickens scratched in the yard. Jacob adjusted his dirndl and glanced at Hans. "This is the house," he said. "There's the bakery two doors down."

They approached the little cottage, and the children paused in their games to regard them with interest coupled with suspicion. *"Guten tag,"* Hans greeted them. "Is this where Peter lives?"

The oldest boy stood up. "I'll get Papa," he volunteered. He returned almost immediately, followed by a thin, balding man with a worried countenance.

"Lars sent us," Hans said uncertainly.

A friendly smile suddenly brightened the man's face. "Come in, come in!" he cried warmly, his suspicions evaporating. "You are welcome here."

He led the way across the sagging porch and into the house. The three travelers followed him uncertainly, but the children were obviously delighted to have visitors and crowded after them eagerly. "Rosalie," the man called, "we have guests."

A thin, tired-looking woman stepped into the room, wiping her hands on a grimy apron. She brightened when she saw the trio, then hurried forward to greet them.

"Our friend Lars sends them," the man informed her, and her eyes widened in surprise. "I am Peter," their host said simply, "and this is my wife, Rosalie." He indicated his children with a broad sweep of his hand. "And these are my children. Marcus is the oldest, then Gustav, and Gretchen, and—" He stopped, clapping his hand to his forehead in mock dismay. "And I never can remember the name of our little one," he teased, his dark eyes twinkling.

He held his finger to his lip, studying the tiny tyke with amusement. "*Ja, ja,* it's . . . uh . . . I have it! Hilda!"

The four-year-old stood, indignantly placing her tiny hands on her hips, her eyes flashing. "Papa!" she sputtered, "you know my name!"

The man held up one finger. "*Nein,* that's not right," he corrected himself. "It's not Hilda. It's . . . uh . . . it's Gunther! *Ja, ja!* Gunther!"

"Papa! I'm not a boy!"

"Huh?" He frowned down at her, feigning surprise, then shook his head. "That's still not it, huh?" He scratched his head, appearing to be deep in thought. "I give up. Who are you?"

"Papa, you know my name!"

"*Ja,* love, but you don't," he teased.

"I do so."

"Then what is it?"

"Anna."

Peter grinned at his guests. "*Ja,* and this is Anna. How could I forget?"

The visitors laughed at the foolishness, suddenly feeling relaxed and right at home without even realizing it. "I'm Hans," the tall boy said. "This is my sister, Gretchen, and this is our friend, who likes to be called Monique."

Peter shook their hands warmly. "It's good to have you."

Anna gravely extended her hand to Jacob. "Good to have you, Neek." Laughter filled the little house.

Rosalie turned to her husband. "Why don't you make our guests comfortable," she suggested, "while I begin dinner." She hurried from the room.

Three extra places were set at the long, narrow table that evening. Gretchen and Monique sat side by side on one side of the table with Gustav and Marcus, while Hans was seated across from them between the second Gretchen and lively little Anna. Hans noticed again that there were benches instead of chairs. He knew without asking that this poor but friendly family were also part of the Underground.

Peter led in prayer and then began to ladle broth into heavy earthen bowls. Anna laid her curly blond head against Hans's arm. "We have *leberknodlsuppe* all the time," she informed him, " 'cause it's good for us."

Hans smiled and ran his fingers through her golden curls. "I like *leberknodlsuppe*," he told her.

The steaming bowls were passed around, and the room suddenly grew quiet as nine hungry people devoured the meal. Hans sighed in satisfaction. "Your mama makes a good *leberknodlsuppe*, Anna," he told the little girl beside him.

She nodded in agreement.

A loud knock at the front door startled everyone. Peter leaped to his feet. "Quickly," he whispered to his guests, "into the pantry."

He threw open the louvered doors behind the table. "Quick! There isn't time to hide elsewhere. I'll get the door."

ESCAPE TO LIECHTENSTEIN

Hans, Gretchen, and Monique gathered their bowls and eating utensils without even thinking about it. The drills at Lars's home had paid off. They scurried into the tiny pantry, noting that the children automatically scooted over to fill the empty spaces left on the benches. As Rosalie closed the door upon them, they heard her husband open the front door.

Moments later, three Nazi soldiers rushed into the room, thrusting the hapless Peter before them. He sat down weakly in his chair. Three terrified young people watched through the slats in the pantry door.

"We're looking for three Jewish children," the leader of the soldiers snarled. He was a big man, powerfully built, with a handsome face. But his features were twisted with rage and hatred, and he reminded Hans of a demon.

"Where are they?" he demanded, shaking Peter roughly by the shoulder.

Peter shrugged, his lips compressed in a thin line. He wasn't telling. In the pantry, Gretchen gasped, realizing what was about to happen to the kind, fun-loving father of four lively children. And it was all on their account. They had brought the Nazi danger upon this innocent family. She reached for the doorknob, but Hans grabbed her hand and shook his head.

"You'll talk, you will!" The burly soldier raised his fist to strike Peter. And then his gaze fell upon Anna.

He lowered his hand. "Come here, little girl," he coaxed, his voice suddenly smooth and gentle. "I want to talk to you."

Her mother's eyes flashed angrily, but she said nothing. Anna walked obediently over to the soldier, who squatted beside her. To everyone's amazement, she climbed upon his knee and put a tiny arm around his thick neck.

"I need to know something," he said quietly. "And you'll tell me, won't you?"

Anna nodded in agreement. "*Ja,* Herr Soldier."

"Were there three children in the house?" Hans saw Rosalie stiffen slightly at the question. He glanced back to Anna, and, to his horror, saw her nod again. They were about to be discovered. "Are they here now?" Again, the curly little head nodded.

"Will you show me where they are?" the big Nazi asked softly.

"*Ja,* Herr Soldier." The little girl climbed down from the man's knee and marched triumphantly toward the pantry!

CHAPTER ELEVEN
THE ARREST

Panic-stricken, the three young people in the pantry held their breath as Anna walked toward them with a happy smile on her angelic little face. Fear gripped them. They were about to be betrayed to the merciless Nazis by the innocent enthusiasm of a four-year-old!

Anna's mother, Rosalie, watched her little daughter in horror. Her eyes pleaded with Anna to stop, but she dared not say anything. The rest of the family sat quietly awaiting the inevitable.

The little girl circled around behind the table, heading for the pantry. But when she reached the pantry door she stopped, and to the amazement of the entire family, turned around and faced the table. "This is one children," she announced, reaching up to lay a small hand on her brother Gustav's shoulder, "and this is two children." She placed her other hand on Marcus's shoulder. Aware that she had the full attention of everyone in the room, Anna played her little drama for all it was worth. It was obvious that she was thoroughly enjoying the unusual opportunity to be the center of attention, and she was going to make the most of it. She marched proudly around the other side of the table to place a hand on her sister Gretchen. "And this," she announced grandly, "is three children!"

Two of the soldiers exploded in laughter. Their leader glared at them in fury, but it made no difference. The men laughed until their shoulders shook, their faces grew red, and the tears ran down their faces. Peter looked from one soldier to another, glanced at his wife, then let out a snicker. As he joined in the laughter, his wife began to laugh, and then the children. The room erupted in laughter.

Little Anna stood in the center of the room with a look of delight on her face and clapped her hands.

Red-faced, the burly Nazi leader glared at his companions, who by now were wiping their eyes. "Enough!" he roared. "Come! Let us be gone!" Without a backward glance, the three Nazis marched from the house.

Peter held up one hand in the direction of the pantry as a silent signal for the fugitives to remain in hiding. Five minutes passed. Finally, he stood to his feet and quietly slipped out the back door. He returned in a few moments, being careful to bolt the front and back doors before he returned to his seat.

"You may come out now," he said quietly, and his simple statement was greeted with audible sighs of relief. "They are gone," he said softly. "God's name be praised!" When Hans, Gretchen, and Monique had returned to their seats, Peter bowed his head and offered a simple prayer of thanksgiving.

After supper, the gentle man led his three guests to a small room in the back. "It is not safe for you to sleep in the house tonight," he told them softly. "I think you'll agree. The Nazis may return at any moment."

He lowered his voice. "There is a small root cellar below the house," he continued. "It is cold and damp, but it is an excellent hiding place. The children do not even know it is there. After they are down for bed, I will show you the way." His visitors nodded.

A short while later, the last of the children were in bed, and the little house was finally quiet. Motioning for the three fugitives to follow him, Peter led them back into the kitchen, then posted his wife at the door to guard against the sudden entry by any of the children.

ESCAPE TO LIECHTENSTEIN

Peter knelt on the kitchen floor beside the table and rolled up the small braided rug that the Nazi leader had stood upon earlier that evening. Hans, Monique, and Gretchen were amazed to see the outline of a trapdoor in the floorboards. A large brass ring was recessed into the wood, and Peter lifted it and gave a sharp tug. With a groan of protesting hinges, the door swung upward.

Peter lit a lantern, adjusted the wick, and then descended the short flight of creaking wooden stairs. Hans and Monique followed their host down eagerly, but Gretchen held back uncertainly.

Peter set the lantern on the earthen floor, and the boys looked about them. The room was tiny, perhaps two by three meters. Dampness hung in the air, and a musty, stale odor pervaded. There were huge gaps in the stonework of the walls, and evidence of rats was everywhere.

The man shrugged. "As I said, it's not fancy, and it's a mite damp and chill. But Rosalie will bring warm blankets, and I think you'll make out just fine. At any rate, the Nazis will never find the place, and you can sleep without worrying."

Gretchen staggered down the stairs, burdened under a huge pile of threadbare blankets. The boys rushed to help her.

"I think it would be best if you start out before daylight," Peter continued. "I'll rouse you before sunup, and we'll have a quick breakfast before you start out."

He put a foot on the bottom stair, then paused as Monique laid a hand on his arm. He turned to face the boy. "I just wanted to say, *Danke schön*. We have put your family in extreme danger. *Danke schön* for helping us."

Peter shrugged. "That's what we're here for," he said simply, "to trust the Lord and help whomever we can."

His boots clomped hollowly on the stairs, and the trapdoor creaked again as it was lowered into place. Scraping, brushing sounds filtered down through the floor, and the young people realized that Peter had replaced the rug over the trapdoor. When their bedding was arranged to everyone's satisfaction, Hans blew out the lantern. The cellar was dark.

Light streamed down into the cellar, and Hans, Gretchen, and Monique awoke to find Peter standing at the top of the stairs. "Up and about!" he called cheerfully. "Sunrise is just around the corner."

Hans sat up, groaning and rubbing his eyes. "We just went to sleep," he complained.

Their host laughed. "Sorry to disturb you," he said, "but Rosalie has breakfast just about ready. By the time we finish eating, you'll have less than thirty minutes before daylight."

After breakfast, Peter accompanied them to the back door. "Cut through the woods behind the house heading due east. When you come to a fence row, turn and follow it to the left. When the fence runs out, continue in a straight line until you reach the road. You'll find yourself on the south side of town and nearly a kilometer from our place. If the Nazis are watching the house, this will keep them from spotting you."

Rosalie handed Hans a large glass jar. "More *leberknodlsuppe*," she said with a smile, "from last night."

ESCAPE TO LIECHTENSTEIN

Peter stepped close to Hans. "You'll be wanting to go to Serfaus," he said quietly. "It's a good twenty-five kilometers from here. You'll have a long day. Take the road south until you come to the railroad, eight or ten kilometers from here. Follow the tracks west for about four, maybe five, kilometers, until it crosses the river. Watch for sentries at the river crossing. Less than a kilometer past the river a paved road runs east and west. You'll want to take the road west to Serfaus."

He glanced from Hans to Monique to Gretchen. "Be careful. I wish I could tell you a safer route, but there is none. When you get to Serfaus, you'll see the shell of a bombed-out factory on a gentle rise at the north end of town. Half a kilometer due east of that factory is a farm with three ancient silos, all set in a row. That's the place. Just ask for Gunther. God be with you. Auf wiedersehen."

Hans handed Jacob the jar of *leberknodlsuppe,* shouldered the rucksack, and they started out. They walked in silence, huddled close together for the reassuring presence of each other's company. The woods were dark and full of shadows, and it was an ideal time for the imagination to run wild. Each bush and tree, each hollow, each windbreak seemed to conceal a Nazi soldier. But as the trio passed each hiding place, the soldiers vanished. Finally, they reached the road.

A rosy glow in the eastern sky heralded the imminent rising of the sun, and before long, the bright golden rays were driving the chill from the morning air. Jacob paused and removed his disguise, rolling the dirndl and kerchief into a tight bundle. Nearly two hours later they spotted two shining ribbons of steel cutting across the sloping hillside. They had reached the railroad.

Glancing furtively about, they began to follow the tracks westward. They walked between the rails, stepping from one wooden tie to another, carefully avoiding the sticky black blobs of tar. "Keep a sharp eye out," Hans said. "We're pretty conspicuous up here."

After nearly an hour of following the tracks, they came to a gorge where the rails descended a long, steep grade and crossed a swift river on a high trestle bridge nearly a hundred meters long. They knelt in a laurel thicket while Hans studied the bridge through the spyglass. "There's a sentry," he reported. "He's pacing across the tracks on the far end of the bridge."

"How do we get across without being seen?" Jacob asked.

Hans frowned as he lowered the telescope. "I don't know," he said slowly, handing the glass to Jacob. "See what you think."

The Jewish boy studied the trestle for several long moments without speaking. "One thing's for sure," he said, "that bridge is the only way across the gorge."

Hans nodded. "*Ja*. But what do we do about the sentry?"

Jacob raised the glass again, refocused it, then peered through it silently. Gretchen plucked a blade of grass and began to poke at a thin line of small black ants. Finally, Jacob lowered the spyglass. "We can cross the tracks right here without too much risk," he told the others. "Once we're in the woods, we can slip down the side of the hill right to the edge of the bridge without being seen."

"What good would that do?" Gretchen argued, glancing up from the ants. "We still can't cross the bridge!"

"Perhaps we can," Jacob replied. "There's some sort of pipe running along the left side of the trestle, about a meter and a half below the tracks. If we can cross on that, we'd be out of sight of the sentry."

Hans stared at him. "We'd be taking an awful risk. That gorge must be sixty or seventy meters deep!"

Jacob nodded. "*Ja,* but it's the only way across that I can see."

Twenty minutes later they crouched at the edge of the woods. Fifteen meters of open ground separated them from the bridge. Hans studied the sentry again through the glass. "We'll have to time it just right," he told Jacob and Gretchen. "He takes fifteen paces in this direction, then fifteen back. When I say go, run as fast as you can to the concrete abutment. Once you reach it, you'll be out of his sight. I'll come on the second pass."

Just over a hundred meters away, the lone sentry paced in their direction. His eye to the spyglass, Hans counted the soldier's steps. "Twelve, thirteen, fourteen, fifteen, ready, go!"

Just as the Nazi turned, Gretchen and Jacob leaped from their hiding place and dashed down the slope, their shoes crunching in the gravel of the railroad bed as they reached the safety of the bridge abutment. Hans noted with satisfaction that they reached the bridge on the sentry's twelfth step. Three paces to spare. He watched the soldier on the return, then snapped the glass closed and dashed to join the others.

"That was the easy part," Jacob told Hans as he joined them. "Look down there."

Hans stared beneath them. The side of the chasm dropped abruptly sixty or seventy meters. Far below, the river foamed white as the surging water boiled and frothed over submerged rocks. An iron pipe less than two handbreadths in diameter hung from steel supports just below the steel girders that supported the tracks. If they could make their way down to the pipe, they could cross the chasm. The girders would be just within reach, and the travelers could use them to steady themselves and maintain their balance. But it would be risky.

"What do you think?" Jacob asked.

Hans shrugged. "We don't have any other choice." Taking a deep breath, he crawled to the edge of the abutment, lowered himself over the edge, then wrapped his legs around a support rod and slid down to the pipe. He planted his feet solidly on the pipe, keeping a tight grip on the vertical rod with both hands. "Gretchen, you're next," he called softly.

He prayed as he watched his trembling sister back slowly over the edge. "Easy now," he encouraged. "Wrap your legs around that steel rod you feel with your feet. Slide down slowly. I'm right below you." A moment later, she landed beside him, her face ashen.

Hans hugged her. "You were great," he whispered. "Now, let's move over for Jacob."

The Jewish boy slid down quickly. "Whose idea was this anyway?" he asked, attempting to take their minds off the fear they felt at being suspended so high in the air. "I don't think I like this."

Hans attempted a weak chuckle. "You go first," he suggested to Jacob. "Gretchen will follow you, and I'll be right behind her."

Jacob started across, carefully sliding one foot after the other along the narrow pipe. He leaned to the right, clutching the steel girder above him with both hands. Gretchen followed, with Hans right behind her. He kept one hand on the girder, the other on his sister's shoulder to steady and reassure her. "Don't look down," he cautioned.

Jacob stopped after twenty meters. He was breathing hard, and his face was pale. "This is scary," he whispered as the others caught up.

"Let's go back," Gretchen urged. "We can't make it."

"We have to go on," her brother whispered. "There's no other way! You can do it. Trust the Lord. We've already come about a fifth of the way."

ESCAPE TO LIECHTENSTEIN

Taking a deep breath, Jacob started again, and the others followed. He stopped again above the center bridge support, clutching a pipe support with both hands. "We're halfway there," he whispered, as Gretchen and Hans caught up. "We need to be very quiet as we get close."

Five minutes later, the three fugitives sighed in relief as they reached the other side. They stood in silence, catching their breath and waiting for the pounding of their hearts to subside. Hans pointed to the gravel embankment below. "If we drop down there," he suggested in a low whisper, "we can slip under the bridge and into the woods without being seen." Jacob nodded in agreement.

Hans knelt on the pipe, placed both hands in position, and dropped over the edge. He was dangling from the pipe, his feet less than a meter above the embankment. He dropped lightly to the gravel, and the others quickly followed.

The sun was sinking fast, and the shadows were growing long as they walked timidly through the narrow streets of Serfaus. Jacob adjusted his kerchief and brushed the blond curls away from his face. "Watch for the factory on the hill," he said. "It should be just ahead."

Gretchen glanced at the dark storm clouds gathering overhead. "We'd better hurry," she suggested. "There's a big storm coming."

"There it is!" Hans said, pointing up the hill. "Look! And there's the farm with the three silos."

At that moment, an elderly man brushed past them on the street. He shoved a folded scrap of paper into Hans's hands. "Read this," he urged, then hurried past.

Hans stared after the old man in surprise and then unfolded the paper. His face registered his shock as he read the note.

"What is it?" Jacob asked in alarm.

"Your contact has been arrested by the Gestapo," Hans read aloud. "Do not stop." He whirled about, but the old man was gone.

"We've lost contact with the Underground," he said slowly. "We're on our own again." Stunned by the message, the three travelers stared at each other in horrified silence.

CHAPTER TWELVE
SECRET DOCUMENTS

Dark, ominous storm clouds closed in over the village, and thunder rumbled threateningly in the distance. The wind gusted and howled, driving stinging sand and dust before it. A few large drops of rain splattered down, and then a brilliant flash of lightning split the sky. Gretchen crowded close to Hans as a blast of thunder rocked the valley.

The three disheartened young people hurried through the suddenly deserted streets of Serfaus. The storm increased in fury, and soon they were thoroughly drenched. "What do we do now?" Gretchen shouted above the din of the storm.

"We don't dare go near Gunther's farm," Hans replied. "I say we need to get as far away from here as possible."

They hurried through the storm. By now it was completely dark, and only the occasional flashes of lightning illuminated their path. Jacob dashed for the shelter of a giant elm. "Over here!" he called to the others. When the next flash of lightning showed them the way, they quickly joined him, cold, wet, and shivering.

"We can't travel all night," the Jewish boy pointed out. "We need to find some place to get out of this storm."

A series of lightning bolts followed one after another in a dazzling display of fiery power, and Gretchen covered her ears as the loud reports of thunder shook the earth. The lightning flashed again, a brilliant, prolonged flash that lasted several seconds. "Look!" Hans called, pointing across the road. "There's a corn field. It would provide us a little shelter and be a safe hiding place for the night."

As the next bolt of lightning streaked across the heavens, the three soaked, shivering young people dashed into the field. The corn was ready for harvest, and the brown stalks towered over their heads. Hans pushed his way to the center of the field with Gretchen and Jacob close behind. They trampled out a little cave-like space between the rows of corn and began to uproot whole stalks and pile them on top. When they finished, the resulting shelter afforded them a small amount of protection from the violence of the raging storm. They crawled in gratefully, huddling together for warmth.

Hans opened the rucksack and removed their extra clothing. He passed the items around, and they slipped the garments on over their wet clothing. "I'm still cold," Gretchen complained, her teeth chattering.

Hans nodded miserably, drawing her closer to him. "It's going to be a long night," he observed. "Here, take my coat."

She snuggled against him but pushed the coat away. "You keep it," she insisted. "You need it as much as I do."

The storm continued to rage. Rain ran down the roof of their makeshift shelter and dripped in on them, but at least they were partially sheltered from the full force of the storm.

Hans rested his chin on his knees. "I don't understand it," he muttered. "It's as if the entire Nazi army is following us. We're constantly just half a step ahead of them. Why are they so interested in us?"

Jacob raised his head, trying to see his friend's face in the darkness. He cleared his throat. "I guess it's time I told you the whole truth," he said quietly. "You two are in this pretty deep, and you've proven yourselves to me again and again."

A bright streak of lightning flashed just then, and the others could see the dismal look on his thin face. They waited silently for him to continue.

"I did tell you the truth," Jacob protested, as though he were fighting with his own conscience. "I am a Jew, and the Nazis are after me. But there's a lot more to it than that. When I tell you, I think you'll understand why the Nazis have been so determined to find us."

Hans and Gretchen leaned close as he began his story. "My real name is not Jacob Reickhoff," Jacob said softly. "My name is Jacob Cohen. My father was a high-ranking officer in the army of the Third Reich, a personal aide to General Reichenbach. Apparently, the fact that he was Jewish did not even matter. Papa was efficient and an excellent officer. He did a lot of outstanding intelligence work for the Nazis.

"But as war loomed on the horizon, Papa began to realize what Hitler and the Third Reich really stood for. He kept his commission, but secretly he became an agent for the Allies and began to work against the Nazis. Holding the position that he did, he was able to secure some very valuable information for the Allies." The Jewish boy paused, and the brother and sister waited expectantly.

"Several weeks ago, Papa came home one evening in a state of agitation and excitement. Mama and my sisters had been sent abroad for their safety, and I was home alone. I was to start schooling the following week in Switzerland."

He sighed deeply. "It happened so suddenly," he said. "Papa came dashing in, grabbed me, then hurried me to his automobile. As he thrust me into the front seat, I saw that he had no driver, which was very unusual. He jumped in beside me, threw the car into gear, then drove as if the armies of hell were pursuing us.

" 'Listen carefully, my son,' he said, continuing to drive like one possessed. 'The Nazis are closing in on me, and I am about to be captured.' Then he told me about his role as a double agent for the Allies. You cannot imagine my great joy at learning that my father was not a Nazi," he said softly. "But there was no time for joy. Papa's life was in danger.

"We drove from the city, and Papa suddenly stopped beside the road in a thick glen of trees. He handed me the map that you have seen me use. 'You must get to the border,' he told me. 'Find Major Von Bronne. He'll know what to do.' "

Hans interrupted. "So why are the Nazis following you," he asked, "if it's really your father they want?"

"They can get to Papa through me," Jacob answered. "If they capture us, they could trade my safety for Papa."

Hans nodded. "I think I understand."

"But that's not all," Jacob continued. "Before I left the car, Papa gave me some valuable documents to carry. He said he figured I had a better chance of making it to the border than he did. I was to give the documents to the Major."

Hans stared at him in the darkness. "So you've been carrying Allied documents this whole time?" he echoed in disbelief. "What are they? And where are they?"

Jacob laughed. "It's all top-secret information," he said. "Papa had sewn it into the linings of my boots. There's a list of twenty-two top-level double agents who are working for the Nazis against the Allies. There's information on the location of several top-secret German munitions factories and plans for a top-secret, underground command post for the führer. The Nazis can't afford for any of the documents to fall into Allied hands."

Hans whistled in amazement. "We're talking some pretty serious stuff!" he exclaimed. "No wonder the Nazis want us!"

Jacob nodded slowly. "I felt that you needed to know before we go any farther," he said. "Now that you know what we're up against, you may want me to go on without you."

Hans shook his head. *"Nein,"* he said, "we're in this together. We'll stick with you all the way to the border." He didn't see the smile of relief that crossed the Jewish boy's face.

Gretchen spoke up. "What happens if the Nazis do catch us?" she asked Jacob.

Jacob wrapped his arms tightly against his chest, trying to stay warm. His teeth chattered as he answered, "We'll undoubtedly be shot on the spot, and the documents will be in their hands."

"And then what?" she questioned.

"I don't know what you are asking," Jacob replied.

"If the Nazis do kill us," Gretchen asked, "what would happen to your soul? Would you go to heaven?"

She couldn't see the frown on his face, but she could hear the anger in his voice as he answered, "I really don't know! I suppose I'd go to hell!"

"You don't have to go to hell," she replied softly. "Jesus died for you."

"You know what I think of your Jesus!" he retorted hotly.

Hans spoke up. "Jacob," he said gently, "Jesus Christ died for the sins of the whole world. That includes you. He loves you and wants to be your Savior, your Messiah, if you'll just let Him."

The cornstalks rustled as Jacob shifted his weight and turned away from Hans and Gretchen. Hans suddenly realized that the rain had stopped. He shivered and drew Gretchen closer to him.

"I'm glad for your help in making this journey," the Jewish boy suddenly said in a strange, distant voice. "I really am. I'm grateful for what you two have done. But I want nothing to do with Jesus. I am a Jew."

CHAPTER THIRTEEN
TRAPPED IN A CAVE

Rain was falling steadily when Hans awoke. He shivered, hugging himself in a futile effort to stay warm. After the long night in the corn field, he was wet, cold, and very hungry. He sat up, brushing against the cornstalks behind him, bringing another shower of cold water down upon himself. He rubbed his eyes and peered about in the dim light. Gretchen was curled up in a dark heap of soggy clothing, still asleep. But Jacob was gone! Alarmed, Hans crawled to the opening in their makeshift shelter and peered out.

A faint glow in the east was beginning to brighten the sky above the forest of cornstalks. Dawn was coming fast, and in another thirty minutes it would be light. Hans suddenly heard a rustling and snapping of cornstalks and spun around. Someone was coming through the cornfield.

To his relief, the corn parted to reveal the lonely figure of Jacob. His arms were folded against his chest as he attempted to keep from dropping the items he was carrying. He pushed his way into the shelter and dumped his load on the ground. Hans gasped in delight. Jacob had brought several bright red tomatoes and a sunny yellow squash. With a proud grin, he then proceeded to unload nine white eggs from his pockets.

Gretchen sat up and rubbed her eyes. She came to life when she saw the food. "Jacob!" she squealed happily. "Where did you get these?"

"Found them in the hen house and in the garden," he answered. "We're near a farm, you know."

She was aghast. "Jacob," she stammered. "You stole them!"

He shook his head. "*Nein,*" he reassured her. "I took a fifty-schilling note from Hans's pocket and left it in the hen house. That farmer has never had such a good price for his crops."

Hans quietly prayed over the food, then picked up two of the eggs. "They're better fried," he observed with a laugh, "but, here goes."

He gently knocked the two eggs together, then opened the shell of the one that cracked, dumping the entire contents into his mouth. The others followed his example. In minutes, the eggs and vegetables were gone.

"We need to head out," Jacob said as they finished. "It is going to be light soon, and we cannot stay here. The farther we get from Serfaus, the safer we will be."

After briefly studying Jacob's map, the trio followed one of the corn rows until they reached the edge of the field. They paused, scanning the area for any signs of life, and then hurried back to the road. Rain continued to fall.

An hour later, the sun finally broke through the clouds. The rain had drizzled to a stop, and the hills to the north were suddenly framed by the colorful splendor of a rainbow. Gretchen pointed to it. "It's going to be a pretty day after all," she observed. "I'm glad for the sunshine."

Jacob pointed to a large outcropping of granite on the side of the hill. "Let's get up on top of that, where we won't be visible from the road," he suggested. "We can dry our clothes."

Moments later, Hans sat behind a bush, enjoying the radiant warmth of the sunshine on his bare skin. His clothes were spread across the face of the rocky ledge behind him drying in the sun. Jacob was close by. On the other side of a dense thicket, some twenty meters away, Gretchen also waited for her clothing to dry.

Hans stood up and walked over to check on his clothes, wincing as the hot surface of the rocky ledge burned his bare feet. He picked up a shirt. It was still damp. He turned each item of clothing over to hasten its drying, then hurried back to the comfort of the cool grass. Yawning, he stretched out again, reveling in the warm caress of the bright sunshine.

He was awakened by Jacob's voice. "Hans! We need to get going." The boys checked their clothing, found the items dry, then quickly dressed. "Gretchen. Are you ready?"

"Nein!" she answered. "Just a minute."

"Well, our clothing is dry, and we're ready to go," her brother replied impatiently. "We're coming over in one minute."

Gretchen was dressed with ten seconds to spare.

That afternoon they paused beside a trickling stream to rest and refresh themselves. Jacob knelt in the grass and thrust his entire head into the water. He came up for air, shaking his head and splashing water everywhere. "That feels good," he laughed.

"Better get your dirndl on," Hans advised. "We're getting near town."

Jacob complied. As he was tying the kerchief on his head, he glanced over at his friend. "Hans," he cried. "What's wrong?"

Hans swayed uncertainly, clutching at his stomach. His face was pale, and he was breathing deeply, as if he was in tremendous pain. "I-I don't know," he answered weakly. "I don't feel so good." He stumbled toward the stream, then suddenly sank to his knees and began to vomit. Gretchen and Jacob looked at each other in alarm and then dashed to his side.

Hans waved them away. "I'll be all right in a moment," he protested. "Just leave me alone for a while."

But he began to vomit again. When he was finished, he was so weak and dizzy he could hardly stand. Jacob helped him to a seat on a nearby rock. "Rest a while," he told Hans gently. "You'll be all right in a little bit."

But as time went by, Hans grew worse. He slid to the ground and leaned his back against the rock, bracing his hands against the ground to steady himself. "It feels like the whole world is spinning," he said to his companions. "I can't travel like this."

Gretchen and Jacob helped him to a grassy knoll out of sight of the road. Hans stretched out gratefully. Leaving Gretchen to watch over her brother, Jacob began to scout the area.

He was back in minutes. "Up here," he called. "There's a perfect hiding place!"

Together, Jacob and Gretchen helped Hans up the steep slope, pausing to rest on an occasional rocky spur. Hans was pale and trembling by the time they had climbed a hundred meters. "It's not much farther," Jacob encouraged him.

Jacob let Hans slide to the ground beside a twisted, gnarled persimmon tree whose leafy branches hung nearly to the ground. With a proud grin, the Jewish boy pulled the branches aside to reveal a dark opening in the rocky face of the mountain. "It's a cave," he cried excitedly. "It's dry as a bone, and soldiers could pass within five paces and never see it."

"How did you find it?" Gretchen asked.

"A squirrel showed me," Jacob explained. "He ran behind the persimmon tree and disappeared. When I followed him, he darted up the face of the cliff. But I spotted the opening when I was poking around in the branches for him." He stepped back to Hans. "Come on, Gretchen, let's get him inside."

They struggled to help Hans into the cave. The opening was just over a meter from the ground, a narrow fissure in the rocks just wide enough for a human body to slip through. Gretchen climbed up first, and then Jacob pushed and lifted Hans up to her. Together they finally squeezed him through the narrow opening.

Gretchen and Hans looked about. Just inside the entrance, the cave widened into a spacious room with a high vaulted ceiling. The floor sloped slightly toward the back of the cave but was dry and sandy.

Hans groaned as they helped him to a reclining position. "Stay with him," Jacob said. "I'll be right back." He scrambled from the cave as Gretchen tried to help her brother get comfortable.

Jacob was back shortly, piling small pine branches in the mouth of the cave, then disappearing for more. Gretchen walked over to the entrance and dragged the pleasant smelling branches deeper into the cave. Jacob brought another load and climbed up to help Gretchen arrange them into a bed for Hans. They completed the project by covering the layer of pine needles with extra articles of clothing from the rucksack. Then they rolled Hans onto the makeshift bed. He groaned softly, still clutching his stomach.

Gretchen and Jacob sat side by side, watching Hans and pondering their predicament. "We have the perfect hiding place," Jacob said finally. "Now all we need is food and water. From Hans's appearance, I'd say we'll be here for a few days."

Gretchen stood up. "I'll go for food," she said. "I'll take some of the money Lars gave Hans."

Jacob shook his head. "I'll go," he said firmly. "I can't let you run the risk."

"And it'll be safer for you, I suppose!" Gretchen shot back. "You're the one the Nazis are searching for, not me."

"She's right, you know," Hans groaned. "You're Jewish, but she's not. It'll be far safer for her to go."

The Jewish boy nodded. "*Ja,* I suppose you're right," he conceded.

Gretchen pulled the roll of bills from her brother's pocket, selected two fifty-schilling notes, and replaced the rest of the money. Hans groaned and rolled over.

"Take care," Jacob told her, worry written on his thin face. "Don't answer any questions. And watch that you are not followed."

She laughed. "I can take care of it," she replied. With a cheerful wave of her hand, she turned and climbed down from the cave.

She returned in less than an hour, thrusting a flour sack up into the entrance to the cavern, then scrambling up after it. Hans rolled over and watched her. His head was pounding, and his face felt flushed and feverish. Jacob walked over to meet Gretchen, and she handed the flour sack to him. "How's Hans?"

Jacob shook his head. "He's pretty sick," he answered. "He vomited a couple of times while you were gone." He opened the flour sack and glanced inside. "You did all right."

She nodded. "I found a tiny, run-down market about a kilometer from here. It was a dirty little place, but at least they had a little food to sell."

"Are you sure you weren't followed?"

Gretchen shrugged. "I was careful. Quit worrying." She knelt beside her brother. "He's got quite a fever," she observed, laying her hand on his forehead. "He's burning up."

"He needs water," Jacob answered, "but I have no idea how to bring it up from the stream." Suddenly he froze, held a finger to his lips, and tiptoed to the cave entrance. Slowly, he pushed the persimmon branches aside and peered out, then carefully let the branches spring back into place. He darted back into the cave to kneel beside Hans and Gretchen.

"There's a Nazi soldier coming straight for the cave," he whispered urgently. "I think he saw me. We're trapped, and there's no place to run!"

CHAPTER FOURTEEN
ROLF'S PLAN

Jacob scrambled to get into his disguise. "Hide," he called to Gretchen. "Get to the back of the cave, behind a rock or something." He slipped the dirndl over his head and smoothed it out, neglecting to fasten the buttons in the back. Frantically, he grabbed the kerchief and whipped it over his head. His fingers flew as he tied a hasty knot.

Her face ashen with terror, Gretchen dashed for the shadows at the rear of the dimly lit cavern. She threw herself behind a smooth, waxlike clump of rock, striking her head on the rocky floor. She struggled to a kneeling position and began to pray fervently.

"*Guten tag!* Who's in there?" Jacob was smoothing the curls over his forehead when the soldier appeared in the doorway of the cave. The daylight was behind him, so he appeared to Hans as a dark silhouette. "Who's there?" the man called again. He entered the cavern, and Hans was surprised to see that he was just a teenager.

"What do you want?" Jacob challenged. The tall, lanky intruder hesitated, glancing from the small girlish figure before him to the motionless form on the cave floor. He looked back at Jacob. "Where's the girl?"

Jacob held his hands in front of him, palms up. "Girl?" he echoed. "What girl?"

"The other one," the Nazi answered. "The one with the long braids, in the blue dress."

"There is no other girl here," Jacob lied, "just my brother . . . uh, Wilhelm, and I. What do you want?"

"The girl came in here," the other insisted. "I followed her."

Gretchen leaped to her feet and emerged from the shadows. "Why don't you Nazis leave us alone?" she cried shrilly. "We haven't done anything to hurt you! Can't you see that my brother is sick? Can't you? For days you've been hunting us, and we're . . ." She burst into tears. "I hate you!"

The young man in the uniform took a step back and held up his hands, almost as if to defend himself. "Wait," he countered. "I'm no Nazi."

"Then why the Nazi uniform?" Gretchen sniffed. "I suppose you're an Allied soldier, and your uniform is being washed!"

"My name is Rolf," the visitor said. "My mother and I live nearby. My father—" he paused, then grimaced as he said, "My father is a Nazi soldier. But I want nothing to do with him. The Third Reich is wrong. Papa is a traitor to Austria!" The young man flinched as he said the words.

"Then why the Nazi uniform?" Jacob asked.

"It enables me to move about unhindered by the Nazi troops," Rolf explained. "But, believe me, I am no Nazi! See, I have no weapon."

"Why did you come here?" Jacob persisted.

"I saw your friend here at the market," the other replied, indicating Gretchen with a wave of his hand. "One look at her face, and I could tell that she was in some sort of trouble. I didn't dare approach her in the open, so I followed her here to see if I could help."

"How do we know we can trust you?" Gretchen challenged.

Rolf shrugged. "You don't. I have no way of proving that I am who I say I am. You'll just have to take my word for it. After all, you have nothing to lose. I do know the location of your hideout."

"How did you find us?" Gretchen demanded. "This cave is well hidden!"

Rolf laughed, then slicked his brown hair back with his hands. "I found this place when I was just a kid," he said. "I used to come here all the time. It was a good place to be alone. When you disappeared so fast on the side of the hill, I figured you must have found the cave."

He knelt beside Hans. "What's wrong with him?"

"We don't know," Gretchen answered, kneeling beside them. "He just got sick this morning. He's been vomiting, and he has quite a fever."

Rolf nodded. "Mama has a tonic that will fix him up," he said with a grin. "The stuff tastes like something you would feed to the hogs, but it'll put you on your feet in no time."

He looked from Gretchen to Jacob. "Do you have any food?"

"A few things I got at the market," Gretchen answered. "Enough for today and tomorrow."

"I'll bring some food with the tonic," the tall teenager promised. "Anything else you need?"

"We need something to carry water from the stream," Jacob replied.

Rolf nodded. "I'll be back this evening," he promised, stepping toward the entrance of the cave. "I'll wait until dusk. It'll be safer." He was gone as quickly as he had come.

Gretchen turned to Jacob. "Do you think we can trust him?"

The boy shrugged. "I guess we don't have much choice," he answered. He looked at Hans. "What do you think?"

Hans grimaced. "I don't know," he said weakly. "But I don't see how we can leave here. I can't even stand up."

"But what if he is a Nazi?" Gretchen worried aloud. "What if he brings the other grenadiers?"

Jacob shrugged again. "We'll just have to wait and see."

Rolf returned that evening. True to his word, he brought food and a gourd to carry water from the stream. He handed Jacob the items, climbed down from the cave, and scrambled back up with three blankets. The three fugitives were delighted. "It's a good thing I wasn't stopped," Rolf commented, placing the folded blankets neatly atop a rock. "I would have had a hard time explaining all this."

He slipped a rusty steel canteen from his belt and handed it to Gretchen. "For your brother," he explained.

She turned it over, noting with displeasure that it was German issue and thrust it back at him. "It's Nazi!" she snarled. "He wants nothing to do with it."

But the teenager handed it back. "Give it to him," he insisted. "He needs it!"

She wrinkled her nose. "What is it?"

"Mama's tonic," he said proudly. "It tastes like it would kill a horse, but Mama swears by it. I've lived through countless doses." He picked up the gourd and headed for the entrance. "I'll get some water from the stream."

Hans was sitting up when Rolf returned. He recoiled at the sight of the Nazi uniform, and Rolf chuckled. "Sorry," he said. "It may take a while to get used to seeing me in this."

It suddenly occurred to Gretchen that no one had been properly introduced, and she promptly introduced Jacob, Hans, and herself.

Rolf nodded at the introductions. "You're the ones the Nazis are searching for," he said.

Jacob stared at him. "How do you know?"

"The Gestapo has been conducting house-to-house searches every few days," Rolf said soberly. "They are offering a reward of ten thousand schillings for your capture. I don't know why they want you so badly, but they're serious about finding you. The country is crawling with Nazis searching for you three."

"That's good to know," Jacob said bitterly.

Rolf handed the gourd to Gretchen, and she helped Hans sit up and take a long drink. He thanked her, then lay back down. Rolf picked up the canteen and handed it to Gretchen. "Get him to drink just a swig of this," he said.

The girl unscrewed the lid and sniffed the contents of the canteen. "Ugh!" she grunted. At her coaxing, Hans sat back up and took a drink of the tonic.

"Yah!" he snorted, wrinkling his face in disgust. "What was that?"

"Just a tonic that Rolf brought us," his sister replied with a grin. "He says it will make you better."

"I'll get better right now, if it means I don't have to drink any more of that miserable tonic!" Hans declared. "Hogs wouldn't drink that!" The other three grinned at each other.

"He's getting better already." Rolf chuckled as Hans lay down.

Rolf suddenly grew serious. "I thought of something this afternoon," he said to Jacob and Gretchen. "My aunt and uncle live in Kappl, which is some twenty kilometers west of here. You can trust them, and they would be more than willing to help you."

"How do we find them?" Jacob asked.

"The road to Kappl crosses a railroad just before it gets into town," the lanky teenager answered. "Uncle Heinz lives on a small farm just across from the rail signal. You'll see a huge haystack right out beside the road, at the very corner of his property. You can't miss it. At least you'd have a safe place to spend the night."

He looked from Gretchen to Jacob. "Use extreme caution," he told them. "Don't go back into town. I'll come by again tomorrow morning and see if there is anything you need."

"I think we can trust him," Gretchen announced to Jacob and Hans when Rolf was gone.

Jacob nodded.

"I think God sent him to us," she continued.

To her surprise, he nodded again. "Perhaps He did," he replied thoughtfully. He glanced at the quiet form of Hans, assumed that he was asleep, and then turned back to Gretchen. "Let me ask you something. It's about God."

They talked long into the night. Jacob asked question after question. He wanted to know what Christians believed about God, about Moses, and especially about Jesus Christ. Hans lay quietly listening, amazed at how open the Jewish boy seemed to the Gospel. He no longer seemed so abrupt and belligerent. Hans prayed as Gretchen answered Jacob's many questions.

Finally, Jacob lay down and wrapped a blanket around his slender form. "Good night, Gretchen."

"Good night, Jacob."

Moments later, Jacob quietly slipped out of the cavern. Gretchen rolled over and lightly touched Hans on the shoulder. "Hans," she whispered, "are you awake?"

"I am now," he replied. "What do you want?"

"I was just talking to Jacob about the Lord," she replied enthusiastically, "and he really listened! He—"

"I heard it," Hans cut in. "I was awake."

"Won't that be special if he gets saved?"

"He might," her brother replied, "if your attitude doesn't drive him away from the Lord."

Gretchen was shocked. "What do you mean?"

"Jacob knows how much you hate the Nazis," Hans explained. "What if that somehow keeps him from coming to the Lord?"

"Why shouldn't I hate them?" she argued. "They killed Mama! And now, they want to kill Jacob, and he hasn't hurt anybody. And they'd kill you and me if they could catch us." Hans couldn't see her face in the darkness, but he heard the raw edge of determination in her voice. "I'll always hate the Nazis. I have the right to hate them!"

"Fine," Hans answered, "but don't let your hatred keep Jacob from seeing that he needs Jesus as his Messiah." The Jewish boy entered the cavern just then, and Hans and Gretchen fell silent. In moments, all three were asleep.

Rolf returned early the next morning. As he entered the cave, he noticed that Hans was sitting up, sipping water from the gourd, and preparing to eat a small amount of food. "You're looking better already," he commented.

Hans nodded. "I still feel weak," he replied, "but I feel a lot better than yesterday."

Rolf glanced at the others. "How did you sleep?"

"Not bad, thanks to the blankets you brought," Gretchen responded.

The friendly teenager smiled. "Glad to help." He leaned forward eagerly. "An idea hit me last night," he said, his voice tinged with excitement. "You're heading for the Swiss border, right?" Jacob nodded warily. "Suppose I drive you there? If we leave in the morning, we could be there by early afternoon."

"Where are you going to get an automobile?" Hans asked.

Rolf waved one hand casually. "Don't worry about that," he laughed. "I can take care of it."

He glanced at Jacob. "You need to head for Liechtenstein," he continued. "Whatever you do, don't cross directly into Switzerland. The Swiss-Austrian border is so heavily patrolled, you'd never make it."

Jacob nodded in agreement. "We planned to hit the border at Schellenburg, cross Liechtenstein, then cross the Rhine at Salez."

"*Gut!*" Rolf responded. "Exactly as I would do it! The Liechtenstein border is not guarded as closely as the Swiss border. If you use caution, you can make it through."

He looked at Hans. "Think you'll be up to a five-kilometer hike tomorrow?"

Hans nodded.

"I'll come for you at first daylight," the enthusiastic youth told them. "We'll have quite a hike, but then we can ride in style. Liechtenstein is just eighty kilometers from here. I'll have you there by noon."

As he left the cavern, the three fugitives chattered excitedly. "It's too good to be true," Gretchen said happily. "Just think, Jacob, tomorrow night you can sleep in peace, knowing you're out of reach of the Nazis."

ESCAPE TO LIECHTENSTEIN

The sun darted behind the clouds as the four exhausted young people paused to rest on the side of the ridge, their keen eyes surveying the Nazi installation in the valley below. The five-kilometer hike Rolf had promised turned out to be the roughest five kilometers that the three fugitives had yet encountered. But, as their cheerful guide had pointed out, they had saved themselves nearly ten kilometers of walking by traversing the rugged landscape instead of following the road.

They studied the Nazi encampment with interest. Row upon row of tanks, jeeps, armored personnel carriers, and other military vehicles, all bearing the swastika and other Nazi insignia, were housed within the perimeter of an eight-foot wire fence, the top of which was draped with coils of barbed wire. Two tall, windowless warehouses stood at one end of the compound, their huge bay doors partially open. Uniformed men swarmed like ants, and sentries regularly patrolled the fenced perimeter. At the gate, two guards stood with their backs to the guardhouse, their machine guns cradled in their arms.

The sun peeked from behind the clouds again, brightening the hillside with its warm, friendly rays. Rolf pointed to a row of long, black automobiles parked near the front gate, their polished windshields reflecting the morning sun. "The second sedan from the end is papa's automobile," he told them. "He gave it to the Nazi regime."

With a grin, he reached in his pocket and then dangled a set of keys in front of them. "We are going to use Papa's automobile," he told them. "I have the spare keys."

Jacob stared at him in alarm. "What are you planning to do?"

Rolf evaded the question. "Stay here until I bring the auto through the gate," he instructed them, "then hurry down to the road. I will pick you up at the point where the ridge dips down to meet the road." With a carefree wave of his hand, he was gone.

Hans, Gretchen, and Jacob watched in silence as Rolf reappeared in the valley several minutes later. He boldly approached the guardhouse, saluted the guards, and walked through the gate unchallenged. The three fugitives looked at each other in surprise.

Rolf sauntered down the row of automobiles, stopped at the second one, opened the door, and climbed in. A cloud of gray smoke from the exhaust told the watchers on the hill that he had succeeded in starting the vehicle. The car backed slowly out of line, then accelerated forward, speeding toward the gate.

The guards spun in the direction of the car and raised their submachine guns, barking out an order to halt. But the sedan never slowed. Rolf gunned the vehicle past the guards and rammed the black-and-white-striped barrier, sending pieces of it hurtling through the air.

The chatter of machine guns echoed across the valley, and the horrified young people saw the back window of the sedan explode in a barrage of flying glass. The car skidded sideways in the gravel, then barreled across the roadway and slammed into a tree. The sound of the violent impact would be etched in their memories forever.

Gretchen turned to Hans and Jacob, her face pale with the shock of the horrifying scene she had just witnessed. "He was trying to help us," she stammered.

CHAPTER FIFTEEN
AUNT HILDA

Hans, Gretchen, and Jacob sat silently on the rugged mountain-side, stunned by the tragedy they had just witnessed. They had known Rolf only briefly, but the cheerful teenager had already proven himself to be a real friend, very unselfish and willing to help where he could. They sat with heads bowed, overwhelmed by the shock of his sudden and violent death. Gretchen began to cry silently, tears coursing down her cheeks.

Hans turned to Jacob. "What do we do now?" he wondered aloud.

Jacob glanced at the wrecked car, now surrounded by Nazi guards, steam rising from its radiator. He turned away. "Well," he sighed, "there's nothing we can do for Rolf. We need to press on. I say we head for Kappl, locate Rolf's Uncle Heinz, and notify him of the accident. Rolf seemed sure that he would be trustworthy and that we could spend the night."

He pulled the wrinkled map from his pocket and studied it briefly. Gretchen scooted over beside Hans, wiping her eyes with the heels of her hands. Hans put an arm around her.

An hour later, the trio passed a weather-beaten farm tucked away on the side of a hill overlooking a deep, sapphire-blue lake. Fleecy clouds drifting lazily across the brilliant blue sky were reflected in the mirror surface of the water. While they watched, an osprey folded his wings in a dive toward the lake and then leveled off at the last possible moment. He rose from the water with a struggling fish in his talons.

Hans nodded down toward the farm. "That might be the place to get breakfast. You two stay here. I'll be right back." Jacob and Gretchen sat down in the shade of a fir to rest and wait. Hans jogged down the lane leading toward the barn and was greeted by a barking collie.

He was back in ten minutes. His shirt was bulging mysteriously. He carried a faded shopping bag that had seen better days. "That lady was great," he laughed as he approached them. "I offered her a fifty, but she wouldn't even take it. Look at what she gave me!"

He set the bag down, knelt beside it, and joyfully began to unload the contents on the grass. "*Schoeberl* from this morning's breakfast," he exulted. "Five of them! Fried potatoes. Fresh carrots. And a jar of milk." He opened the bottom of his shirt and Gretchen laughed in delight as a cascade of shiny red apples tumbled out, rolling across the grass in all directions. "She told me to pick all I wanted, so I got a dozen," Hans said gleefully. "Four for each of us."

The distant purr of a motor caught their attention, and they looked up to see a cloud of dust making its way down the road toward them. "Oh, oh," Jacob grunted. "It's a Nazi jeep."

They dropped instinctively on their bellies behind the fir, their faces pressed to the ground. But the jeep didn't slow, and moments later it had disappeared in the distance. Hans gathered the food, stuffing it back in the bag. "I guess we had better find a safer spot for our little picnic," he said ruefully. *"Ja?"*

They hiked to the other end of the lake, slipped to the edge of the woods, then spread the feast upon the grass. The *schoeberl* were excellent, and silence reigned as the three hungry young people enjoyed the delicious meal. "You picked the right meal ticket this time," Jacob said happily, as he reached for a second pancake.

From where they sat, the farm was now reflected in the mirror surface of the lake. Gretchen sighed as she gazed down at the shimmering image of the big red barn, the little stone farmhouse, and the herd of black-and-white Holsteins grazing on the emerald green hillside. "If I were an artist," she said dreamily, "I would come back here and paint this scene. It's beautiful."

Jacob bit into an apple. "I'd paint a still life," he said, his dark eyes twinkling. "A basket of juicy red apples, surrounded by mounds of hot, flaky *schoeberl!*"

Hans studied the farm. "I wonder why the Nazis didn't strike here," he commented. "These people are just about the only ones in all Austria who still have their cattle."

Hans packed the remaining food into the bag as they finished. "We have enough for tonight," he said happily. Content and well fed, they resumed their journey with renewed energy.

The food was gone by the time they reached Kappl. The three weary travelers followed the road into town, Jacob again disguised as Monique. They paused when they came to the railroad.

"Where did Rolf say his uncle lived?" Hans asked. "He said something about it being beside the railroad."

"He told us to look for a haystack across from the railroad signal," Jacob replied. "There's the signal box, and there's the haystack. We've come to the right place." He frowned. "But which farm does the haystack belong to? It looks like it's right on the border between these two farms."

They stood in the road, studying the situation. Sure enough, the haystack in question was equidistant from the two farmhouses. There was no fence dividing the properties, and it was impossible to determine to which farm the hay belonged.

"I'd say it's the farm on the right," Hans ventured. "Shall we give it a try?"

They trooped across the freshly painted porch and timidly knocked on the door of the farmhouse. When there was no answer, Hans knocked a second time. The door suddenly opened to reveal a big, beefy woman with a scowl on her face. *"Ja?"* she boomed.

Hans glanced uncertainly in Jacob's direction, then back to the woman. "Do you have a nephew named Rolf?" he asked, intimidated by the woman's size and stern countenance.

"Who?" the woman demanded.

"Rolf," the boy answered. "We're looking for his Uncle Heinz. Is this the place?"

Suddenly the huge woman was all smiles. *"Ja, ja,* this is the place!" she said bubbling. "Come in, come in," she invited, throwing wide the door. "And how is dear little Rolf?"

She ushered them into the kitchen, waved them each to a seat, and dropped her bulk onto a tiny stool. "So Rolf sent you, did he?" she said.

"Ja, Frau, he did," Hans replied. He paused, then gently told her of the tragic events of the morning. To his surprise, the big woman showed no emotion. She seemed more interested in her visitors.

"And where was he going to take you in the auto?" she asked, her pudgy eyes narrowing.

Hans quickly sidestepped the question. "My name is Hans," he said quickly. "This is my sister Gretchen, and this is a friend of ours. She'd like you to call her Monique."

"Guten tag," their hostess answered. "I'm Rolf's aunt. Now, again, exactly where was Rolf intending to drive you before he was killed?"

Gretchen and Jacob looked to Hans, leaving him to field the tricky question. Hans paused. The woman was watching him closely. He was saved from answering by the sound of boots scuffing on the back porch. The big woman leaped to her feet, moving surprisingly fast for someone her size. "That'll be Heinz, now," she remarked, bustling toward the back door. "I'll let him in."

The door opened, and a foot appeared across the threshold, but the big woman hustled through the door, sweeping whoever was entering back out with her. She closed the door firmly behind her. The young people could hear a faint murmur of voices as she and the other person talked in hushed tones.

"You know what I think?" Gretchen volunteered. "I don't think this is Rolf's aunt at all."

Jacob agreed. "Let's get out of here," he urged.

But at that moment, the door opened again, and the huge woman ushered a thin man into the room. "This is Heinz," she said to her visitors. "Rolf's Uncle Heinz."

Heinz was just the opposite of his wife. Small and quiet, he stood meekly beside her as she introduced each of the young people. He shook hands with each of them nervously.

"And what did dear Rolf tell you about me?" the woman asked after everyone had been introduced.

"He didn't say anything about you, Frau," Gretchen volunteered. "He didn't even tell us your name."

The big woman seemed glad for this bit of information. She relaxed as she said, "Then I'll tell you. I'm Rolf's Aunt Hilda. Perhaps I should tell you, Rolf was our favorite nephew. Isn't that right, uh . . . Heinz?"

The little man nodded uncomfortably. "Dear Rolf had an accident today," Hilda told her husband. While the young people listened in stunned silence, she casually recounted the details of their new friend's violent death. Neither of them showed any emotion whatever during her account of the automobile wreck.

"Well, enough of that," she said cheerfully, wiping her hands on her apron. "Heinz, it is time for the broadcast. Why don't you take our guests into the sitting room so they can listen to der führer with you? I'll be getting supper on."

The little man ushered them to the front room. They took seats while he fiddled with the knobs on the big mahogany cabinet radio. Static filled the room, then the radio bleeped and belched while he adjusted the frequency. Finally, he settled back in his rocker as a harsh, grating voice filled the room.

Hans closed his eyes as a futile defense against the hateful words. He could picture Hitler as he stood before the microphone, ranting and waving his arms, his mustache writhing on his upper lip as he poured forth the venom of Nazism. Hans cringed as he heard the verbal assault on the leaders of the free peoples of the world. The fanatical voice rose in pitch as it promised the destruction of the "imperialistic Allies" under the victorious heel of the invincible Third Reich.

He opened his eyes to discover that Aunt Hilda had entered the room and was watching him curiously. Embarrassed and alarmed, he tried to keep his face from registering his emotions. Finally, the broadcast came to a close, and the woman hurried back to the kitchen as her husband turned off the set.

They sat down to a simple meal of *gulyassuppe, ankerbrot,* and big glasses of dark, bitter tea. "Isn't it glorious," Hilda exulted as they ate, "that der führer chose to allow Austria to become part of the Third Reich? Our future is magnificent under Anschluss. Some day, Austria and Germany will rule the world. Anschluss forever!"

Jacob brushed self-consciously at his blond curls. He pulled the sleeves of his dress lower, trying to hide his trembling hands. Hans noticed his nervousness, and his own doubts were confirmed. *This is not Rolf's Uncle Heinz and Aunt Hilda, and the three of us are in extreme danger every minute we are in the house!*

The kettle on the stove began to whistle, and Hilda set it on the sideboard. She shuffled to the back porch and filled a ten-liter bucket from the pitcher pump, then reentered the house. Lifting the kettle from the sideboard, she gestured with her elbow to Gretchen and Jacob. "Come with me."

Bewildered, Gretchen and Jacob followed her down the short hall. The woman opened a door to reveal a gleaming porcelain tub standing proudly on four cast iron legs. She emptied the bucket into the tub and then poured in the contents of the steaming kettle.

"Strip," she ordered, "then climb in. I can tell you young ones haven't had a bath in a week or two, and I figure it's time you had one. You two girls can bathe together, then Hans gets the tub."

As she stepped into the hall and closed the door behind her, Hans caught a glimpse of Gretchen and Jacob standing beside the tub, staring at one another in astonishment.

CHAPTER SIXTEEN
PURSUED!

Hans sat on the deacon's bench at the end of the hall, straining to hear what was taking place inside the bathroom. He heard a splash and a dull thud as someone sat down in the tub, and his eyes widened in astonishment. Surely Gretchen wouldn't—*nein,* not Gretchen!

But what were Jacob and Gretchen going to do? Hilda was expecting them to take a bath, and if they didn't, her suspicions would surely be aroused. And she and Heinz were already watching them closely.

Moments later Hilda pushed past Hans and knocked on the bathroom door. "Girls," she called, "are you just about through? Hans is waiting."

"Just about!" Gretchen's voice answered. "Monique is getting rinsed off."

Hans stared at the door. *They didn't! Surely they didn't! I can't imagine Gretchen doing such a thing!*

But the door suddenly opened and Gretchen came out, her face as red as a slice of fresh watermelon. Hans noticed that her hair was damp. He stared. "Gretchen," he whispered, "did you—"

"*Nein,* of course not!" his sister whispered fiercely, her face growing even redder. "What did you think we would do? Jacob got a bath while I sat in the corner with my back to the tub, then he did the same for me."

Hans was relieved. "Just thought I'd ask," he replied.

ESCAPE TO LIECHTENSTEIN

Their hostess was waiting in the kitchen with a second kettle of water on the stove. "Fill the bucket," she ordered Hans. "You're next."

The moon rose silently over the hemlock at the edge of the farm, casting silver beams across the fields and farmyards. In the house, the three weary travelers lay side by side on blankets their hostess had rolled out on the kitchen floor. Gretchen and Jacob were drifting off to sleep, but Hans lay on his back, hands beneath his head, his mind racing.

I don't like it, he told himself. *We're in danger here. It's obvious that these people are not loyal Austrians, and we're taking a huge risk just being in this house.*

He rolled over and nudged Jacob. "Hey, you awake?" he asked quietly.

"Uh-uh," Jacob answered drowsily. "Leave me alone."

"Jacob, listen," Hans whispered urgently. "Wake up!"

Jacob rolled toward him. "What's wrong?"

"Maybe nothing," Hans answered. "But I just have this feeling that we're in grave danger. Let's get out of here."

"Nein-n-n," the Jewish boy sighed, his eyelids drooping closed. "Let's go to sleep."

Hans tried again, but his friend refused to be awakened. He finally gave up. Perhaps his imagination was working overtime. So far, Jacob had been so alert and had seemed to be able to sense danger every time. If Jacob was not alarmed, then maybe he needn't be either.

Hans tried to go to sleep, but his mind refused to rest. It was as though a little voice inside was screaming, "Danger! Danger!" He tossed and turned, but it was no use. He just couldn't relax.

Finally, he stood quietly to his feet. He would make one more trip to the outhouse. Perhaps the cool night air would settle his nerves and cause him to relax. He stepped gently over the sleeping form of Gretchen, then tiptoed to the back door. He opened the door, wincing as the hinges groaned in protest. He stood quietly for a moment, but no one stirred.

The back yard was bathed in silver moonlight, and the trees cast long, dark shadows. Hans slipped to the outhouse, and then, moments later, started back to the house. He paused in the yard, gazing up at the brilliant silver moon. The night was peaceful. The war seemed so far away that the terror of capture by the Nazis was like a bad dream. He sighed and started toward the house.

A dog began to bark, and Hans turned toward the sound. Dancing lights on the road caught his attention. Two vehicles were making their way down the lane toward the railroad crossing. He saw the headlights of the first vehicle shoot skyward, then dip toward the ground as the automobile crossed the tracks.

Suddenly, panic seized him. *The headlights on the first auto are close together, as they would be on a jeep! What if the two vehicles are Nazi jeeps? What if they're coming to the farmhouse?* As the second vehicle crossed the tracks, he ran for the house.

His heart racing, Hans slipped silently in the back door. He tiptoed to the front room, drawing the curtains aside to peer through the front window. The first set of headlights slowed, and the vehicle turned into the farmyard!

Hans threw the bolt on the front door and dashed to the kitchen. Kneeling between the inert forms of Jacob and Gretchen, he shook them both by the shoulders. "Jacob! Gretchen!" he whispered urgently, "Wake up! Get up!"

Jacob sat up sleepily. "Huh? Is it morning already?"

"Nein!" Hans whispered fiercely. "Get up. There are Nazis in the front yard."

"Oh," Jacob mumbled, then lay back down. He closed his eyes.

Hans was frantic. He slapped Jacob twice across the face, hard. "Get up, Jacob," he pleaded. "The Nazis are here!"

Jacob sat up, rubbing his eyes, and Hans turned his attention to Gretchen. Placing his hands beneath her shoulders, he lifted her to a sitting position and shook her roughly. "Gretchen, wake up. The Nazis are here!"

At that moment, he heard the front door rattle—then a loud knock. Gretchen leaped to her feet. "Hans," she wailed, "what will we do?"

"Keep your voice down," he whispered urgently. "Go out the back door and run quietly to the outhouse. Stay in the shadows."

She seemed to comprehend and hurried from the room. Hans turned back to Jacob and was relieved to hear, "*Ja,* I'm awake now. Let's go."

They reached the back door just as Gretchen was closing it. Hans latched it behind him, then dashed after Jacob and Gretchen to the shadow cast by the outhouse. "That way!" Hans called softly. "Into the woods."

As the trio slipped into the shadows of the forest, Hans glanced behind them. Four dark figures appeared at the corner of the house and headed for the back door. The terrified boy slowly let out a long breath.

Suddenly, the headlights from one of the jeeps swung across the yard, catching the three fugitives in the bright beams. The brilliant light swung back and stopped. They were trapped in its glare.

"There they are!" a voice shouted. "After them!"

Terrified, the three young people dashed between the trees. Limbs and briars tore at their arms and faces in the darkness. "Stay together!" Hans called. "Follow Jacob!"

Shots suddenly rang out behind them, and they cringed as they heard the whine of bullets cutting through the air. Jacob darted and dodged through the trees, running for all he was worth. Enough moonlight trickled through the branches to enable Hans and Gretchen to keep him in sight, and they did their best to keep up with him. They ran until their lungs burned. Finally, Jacob paused for breath, head down, hands on his knees. The other two caught up, panting and gasping for breath.

Panting heavily, Jacob held up one hand. "Listen," he gasped. Gretchen and Hans held still, listening intently while they tried to catch their breath. The noise of their pursuers had faded, and the only sound they heard was the distant hoot of an owl.

"We've lost them momentarily," Jacob said, "but we've got to keep moving. They know we're in here, and they'll have the woods surrounded before long."

As he spoke, they heard a shout, then saw a searchlight shining among the trees. "Look!" Hans cried. "They're coming from the other direction! They have us surrounded!"

Jacob leaped to his feet. "We've got to keep moving!" he cried. "Follow me! Let's head more to the north. Maybe we can cut around them." More lights appeared, bobbing about between the trees like oversized fireflies, and the woods echoed with men shouting directions and orders. Jacob stopped for a moment, then took off in a different direction. They ran until their sides ached and their lungs screamed for air. Jacob stopped again, and Hans and Gretchen leaned against each other, trying desperately to suck enough air into their tortured lungs.

"It's no use running," the Jewish boy finally panted. "They have us surrounded. If we keep running like this, we'll run right into them. We've got to hole up and hide, if only we can find a decent place." He pushed his way through a thicket, then suddenly dropped out of sight. Gretchen and Hans heard a loud splash.

Hans pushed his way into the bushes, feeling his way along carefully with his foot. He took a cautious step, and suddenly there was nothing but empty air beneath his shoe. He drew back, realizing that he had reached the small precipice over which his friend had fallen. He parted the branches in front of him and spotted Jacob standing in water up to his chest. He had walked right into a small river.

"Gretchen. Hans." Jacob called softly. "Come down here with me. Here's the perfect hiding place."

Hans stepped off the edge and dropped into the water with Jacob. There was little current, and the bottom was rocky and solid. He coaxed Gretchen, and she joined them in the water. "It's cold," she complained.

"Look!" Jacob said excitedly. "The far bank has been undercut by the current, and those bushes help conceal the space underneath. We can hide under there, and the soldiers can't even see us, unless they come down into the water."

Gretchen drew back. "*Nein!* I'm not going under there."

A searchlight cut through the trees, and the sound of running feet passed on the bank right over their heads. "Come on, what are we waiting for?" Gretchen whispered. She waded through the river and ducked into the hiding place that Jacob had pointed out. The two boys were right behind her.

They crouched in the water, watching as several soldiers searched along the banks. Searchlights shone across the water, reflecting off the surface into their faces. But they knew that they were not visible to the soldiers unless the men actually came down into the water with them.

A group of soldiers suddenly appeared on the bank and an authoritative voice called out, "Search the river! I want four men in the water! Look under each log; search out every crevice. They came this way, and we're going to find them!"

Pursued!

Splash! Splash! Four soldiers followed orders, holding their weapons high overhead as they jumped into the shallow river. The resulting ripples lapped against the far bank, splashing the faces of the three frightened fugitives who crouched in the water. The Nazis were in the water with them.

CHAPTER SEVENTEEN
THE BEAVER DEN

The three frightened young people crouched under the bank in the dark river with water lapping at their chins. The soldiers in the water were barely ten meters away and coming closer every second. Hans realized that if a searchlight flashed their way, their hiding place would instantly be discovered. "What can we do?" he whispered.

"I don't know," Jacob whispered back. "Stand perfectly still. Don't make any ripples!"

The soldiers came closer, their searchlights carefully probing underneath the banks, examining each snag in the water, pausing to check each possible hiding place. There would be no escape. The Nazis would find them.

Hans crept backwards, extending his hand farther beneath the bank. To his surprise, his probing fingers discovered a void. Many years before, an animal had dammed up the river and then built its den under the riverbank. The many seasons of flooding had eroded the bank beneath the entrance, and the floor of the entrance tunnel had finally collapsed into the water. Hans had stumbled onto the air pocket that resulted.

"Gretchen. Jacob," he whispered. "I've found an empty space under the bank! Grab my hands. I'll lead you to it."

Jacob went first. He took a lung-full of air, then ducked beneath the surface of the water and came up inside the cavity Hans had discovered. To his amazement, his head was above water. Gretchen followed him, then Hans came last.

They stood in silence, breathing hard. Their hiding place was pitch black and a bit frightening, but it was reassuring to know that they were safe from discovery by the Nazis. Hans spoke first. "I think it's an old den," he whispered, "probably from a muskrat or a beaver. They'll never find us here!"

They stood in silence for fifteen or twenty minutes. They listened intently but could hear no sounds of the soldiers. The little underwater chamber apparently was soundproof. There was no way of knowing what was happening outside their little den.

"We can't stay here all night," Gretchen complained. "I'm cold. And if we fall asleep, we'll drown."

"If you fall asleep," Jacob whispered, "the river will wake you up."

Hans was silent. He had turned around and was busily exploring again in the dark. His probing hands had discovered that the tunnel they were in led upwards from the water. Without saying anything to the others, he crept up the incline on his belly. He found himself in a fairly dry cavern, perhaps two meters in diameter and slightly less than half a meter high. The floor was lined with small twigs and wood chips.

"It's dry up here," he called softly. "Gretchen. Jacob. Come up to where I am."

The others immediately began searching for him. "Where are you, Hans?" Gretchen asked in bewilderment.

"I'm up in some sort of den," Hans laughed. "It's too large to have been a muskrat's burrow, so it must be a beaver den. There's room for all three of us. Turn around and feel your way up the bank behind you."

Jacob finally discovered the incline leading up from the water and led Gretchen to it. In a moment, they had joined Hans in the deserted beaver den. "At least we're out of the water," Gretchen observed. "Now we won't be so cold."

ESCAPE TO LIECHTENSTEIN

The three fugitives were wet, muddy, and cold, but they fell asleep quickly in the coziness of their underground hideaway, secure in the knowledge that the German troops could never find them there. They were safe, at least for the moment.

Hans slowly lifted his head, peering about him in the dim light. Where was he? He shook his head in confusion. Suddenly the events of the night before came rushing back upon him—the terrifying flight through the darkness to escape the pursuing soldiers, the plunge into the river, the just-in-time discovery of the vacant beaver den. He stared about him. So that's where they were now—the beaver den.

He noticed a thin shaft of brilliant light creating a bright splash on his arm, and he craned his neck to discover the source of the light. Many years before, the beaver that had constructed the den had burrowed between the roots that formed the ceiling to create a ventilation shaft for the den. Hans found that the narrow crevice led to the surface, admitting the bright shaft of sunlight. Outside their little beaver den hideaway, the sun was high in the sky.

He nudged the others awake. "Where are we?" Gretchen mumbled, rubbing her eyes and attempting to sit up. She smacked her head on the low ceiling and fell back, startled but unhurt.

Jacob rolled over on his belly. "That was a rough night," he said. "What a place to sleep!"

"*Ja,* but you have to admit, it was a safe place," Hans replied. "We're still alive."

"I'm hungry," Gretchen declared. "And I'm muddy, and my leg hurts. Let's get out of here."

Jacob shook his head. *"Nein,"* he said, "that would not be wise. We are safe here, even if it is a little cramped. It is better to be hungry than dead."

They discussed their situation at length and came to the conclusion that it would be safest to remain in the burrow for most of the day. Hans would leave the den just after sunset to scout the area and, perhaps, find food. If all was clear, they would travel at night.

They spent a long, long day underground. In spite of the small amount of fresh air coming through the ventilation shaft, the air grew stuffy in the close confines of the den. All three were hungry, and they were anxious to be on their way. But they knew the necessity of staying out of sight as long as possible. Now that the Nazi grenadiers had actually spotted them, they would undoubtedly continue the search throughout most of the day.

Finally, the light streaming through the hole grew faint as the afternoon sun dipped toward the western hills. Hans lay flat on his back and pressed his face against the ceiling of their hideaway, trying to peer through the ventilation hole. "The sun's in the west," he reported. "In just a couple of hours, it will be dark. What do you think?"

"We have not heard the soldiers at all today," Jacob replied. "If they were searching the riverbanks, surely we would have heard them on the roof of the den. Perhaps it is safe to venture outside."

"I will go alone," Hans volunteered. "I'll scout out the area, and also see if I can find food. If the coast is clear, I will return for you."

"Use caution," Jacob warned. "The troops may be hiding in the woods."

"Ja," Hans replied, "I will be careful." He squeezed Gretchen's hand for a moment, gave a playful slap at Jacob's shoulder, then slid headfirst down the entrance tunnel. When he reached the water, he gulped a huge lung-full of air, then plunged in.

ESCAPE TO LIECHTENSTEIN

He swam underwater as far as he could. If the soldiers were watching, he did not want to give away the location of the beaver den when he emerged from the water. Finally, lungs burning, he gently floated to the surface.

He was relieved to discover that he had surfaced beneath the overhanging branches of a water fern. The leafy tendrils actually hung down into the water, creating an excellent hiding place. He crouched in the water for several minutes, scanning the area with his eyes, listening intently. All seemed quiet, so he cautiously slipped from the water.

Hans crawled into the dense undergrowth at the water's edge. He lay quietly for several minutes, listening intently. Slowly, carefully, he began to make his way through the bushes. He worked his way toward the top of the hill overlooking the river. When he came to a trail winding through the woods, he paused for a moment, then scurried across it. He dared not take the trail, even though it led in the same general direction he was heading. He could not afford to take any chances.

Hans paused to catch his breath at the top of the hill. Carefully, moving only a few inches at a time, he climbed into the leafy branches of a sweet gum. From here he could survey both sides of the ridge. He glanced down toward the river, then turned his attention to the valley behind him.

He caught himself just in time to keep from uttering a cry of delight. Through the trees, less than two hundred meters away, he caught a glimpse of a brightly-painted red barn. He had stumbled onto a farm! Perhaps there would be food. "Thank you, Lord," he breathed as he silently slid from his leafy perch.

Moments later, Hans lay in the bushes overlooking the quiet farm. A low stone wall circled around behind the barn he had seen from the top of the hill, and on the other side of the wall, a small white farmhouse rested beside a gravel road. Between the house and the barn, on the near side of the wall, lay a vegetable garden. Hans couldn't take his eyes off it. Food! The garden lay before him like a huge green treasure chest, the ripe, colorful vegetables as valuable to him as jewels.

While he watched, a stooped figure in a huge, shapeless hat strode from the barn, passed through the narrow gate in the wall, and entered the house. This was his chance. Hans slipped quickly down the hillside, being particularly careful to keep just inside the edge of the woods until he came to the stone wall. He dropped to his knees and crawled along the edge of the wall until he reached the garden. Glancing furtively about, he knelt in the garden, hurriedly picking the tempting vegetables.

The gate opened so suddenly that Hans was caught by surprise. He dropped flat on his belly behind a row of yellow squash. An elderly man and woman entered the garden, hobbling straight toward him! They hadn't yet noticed his presence, so he quickly shoved his vegetables under the broad, flat leaves of the nearest squash plant, then crawled under the leaves himself.

"Somebody's been in the garden!" the woman suddenly said in a high, thin voice. "Look! They've taken some of my tomatoes!"

"Nein," the man responded, "you're imagining things. Who would have come here?"

"I tell you, somebody's been here," his wife said again. "I can tell. This vine on the end had two of the nicest tomatoes you ever saw. I've been waiting for three days for them to get ripe, and now they're gone. Someone's been in the garden!"

Under the row of squash plants, Hans drew his feet in close and made himself as small as possible. The woman walked down the row and stopped, standing so close he could have reached out and touched her shoe. "There's squash missing too!" she cried.

The old man shook his head. *"Nein!"* he argued. "You're getting old, woman. You can't keep a count of all the food in the garden. You picked it, and you forgot."

Still grumbling, the old woman walked up and down the rows, examining the plants, occasionally picking an item and adding it to the basket on her arm. Her husband weeded around the tomatoes until she was ready to leave.

Hans slowly let out his breath as he watched the gate close behind them. *That was close! I'll have to be more careful. I didn't even hear them approaching.* He quickly gathered his vegetables from under the squash, then sighed as he pulled a damp fifty-schilling note from his pocket and inserted it in the splintery end of a tomato stake. This was the last of the money Lars had given them. Three hundred schillings had been in the rucksack, left behind when they had fled the farmhouse to escape the soldiers.

Twenty minutes later, Hans knelt behind a large bush on the bank of the river, scanning the woods around him. All was quiet. He left the vegetables beneath the bush, then crawled quietly through the tall grass until he located the ventilation hole for the beaver den.

Lying down in the grass, he put his mouth close to the hole. "Gretchen," he called softly. "Jacob. Can you hear me?"

"What took so long?" Gretchen's voice answered. "We've been waiting forever."

"Find anything?" Jacob wanted to know.

"Ja!" Hans answered happily. "I got some vegetables from a farm, and I scouted around just a bit. I think we can safely head west again. Everything seems quiet. Come on out."

Two heads popped up in the river moments later, and Jacob and Gretchen emerged dripping from the water. Hans waved at them from the bushes, and they scrambled to join him. He opened his shirt and handed them some of the vegetables he carried.

"Follow me," he said softly, biting into a carrot. "I saw no sign of the soldiers, but we still need to keep a low profile."

Munching on the food, the three fugitives crept through the woods until they came to a small game trail. "Let's take it," Hans decided. "It heads in the general direction we are going, and it will be far easier than fighting our way through these brambles. I haven't seen a single soldier."

Moments later, he suddenly stopped. "Look," he said to Jacob. "What's this?" He pointed to a round metal disk half-buried in the soil, partially covered by a cluster of green leaves.

As Hans reached for the object, Jacob screamed, "*Nein!* Don't touch it!"

Hans stared at him in alarm.

"It's a *tellerminen!*" the Jewish boy told him. "If you had stepped on it or picked it up, it would have blown us all to pieces."

Still shaking, the three young people stepped gingerly around the explosive device. "We'll have to watch carefully," Jacob warned. "The Nazis may have planted others!"

They had walked another ten or fifteen meters when a voice behind them suddenly commanded, "Halt! Hands in the air!"

They turned around slowly. Stalking down the trail toward them was a grinning Nazi soldier, his machine gun pointed right at them. "We knew we would find you sooner or later," he laughed triumphantly. "No one can escape the armies of the Third Reich!"

CHAPTER EIGHTEEN
JACOB'S DECISION

Hans turned to run, but Jacob grabbed his arm. *"Nein!"* he shouted. "Don't run. He will shoot us all."

The soldier advanced toward the three terrified young people, his machine gun still trained on them. "Come toward me," he ordered.

Hands in the air, Jacob, Hans, and Gretchen turned toward the Nazi, who walked forward to meet them. He laughed at the look of terror on their faces. "You really didn't expect to elude us forever, did you?" he gloated. "Do you know how much your capture means to us?"

At that instant, an ear-shattering explosion blasted through the forest, and the Nazi soldier was thrown nearly three meters into the air. His weapon flew from his hands to land harmlessly in the leaves. He landed on his back in the middle of the trail, his body badly mangled, blood pouring from a number of terrible wounds. A heart-rending scream of pain and terror came from his quivering lips. He had stepped directly on the land mine hidden on the trail.

Horrified, the three young people stared at the dying soldier. His helmet was gone, blown off by the tremendous force of the blast, and they saw a youthful, boyish face. Gretchen ran to him, knelt by his side and tenderly placed a small hand on the young man's bloody cheek.

"Mama!" the soldier cried, delirious with shock and pain. "Mama? Where are you?" He looked up into Gretchen's face, his blue eyes glazed with agony. "Mama? Is that you?"

Gretchen's eyes filled with tears as she answered, "*Nein,* soldier, I'm not your mother. I'm . . ." she swallowed hard, ". . . just a friend."

The young Nazi soldier screamed again in pain; then his head fell back, and he lay still. He was dead. Gretchen stood to her feet, tears streaming down her face, and ran sobbing into her brother's arms.

"Oh, Hans," she wailed, "he was just a boy, like you! Somewhere his mother is waiting, but when the war is over, he won't be coming home."

She suddenly ran back and knelt beside the lifeless body of the soldier. "Dear God," she prayed, her tears falling on the Nazi uniform, "forgive me for hating them. Forgive me!" Her voice fell silent as sobs shook her slender body.

Hans smiled sadly as he watched his sister. For weeks she had been carrying the unbearable burden of bitterness and hatred toward the people who had killed her mother. Finally, she was learning to forgive. He was glad to see that compassion and forgiveness were replacing the bitterness in her heart.

But his thoughts were suddenly shattered by a shouted command that echoed through the forest. He glanced up just in time to see two Nazi soldiers scrambling down the ridge toward them, their guns held high as they dashed through the dense undergrowth.

Hans ran forward and seized Gretchen by the arm. "Come on!" he shouted. "The Nazis are coming!" As the three young people ran frantically down the trail, they heard gunshots, punctuated by the screaming whine of bullets flying overhead. Crouching low as they ran, they left the trail and sprinted into the darkness of the woods.

"Follow me," Jacob called, taking the lead. He turned and scrambled up a narrow gully with Hans and Gretchen on his heels. They raced over the crest of the ridge, then crossed a wide meadow. As Jacob scrambled under a thicket at the far end of the meadow, Hans turned and glanced behind him.

Seven or eight green uniforms burst out of the trees at the end of the meadow. The lead soldier dropped to one knee and fired several quick rounds, then leaped to his feet and raced toward them.

Hans had seen enough. He leaped over the top of the bushes, fell on his face, then scrambled to his feet a step or two ahead of Jacob and Gretchen. They ran desperately through the woods, heedless of the sharp briars and branches tearing at their faces and clothing. Suddenly they heard the chatter of a machine gun, and the fearsome sound urged them to greater speed.

Gretchen tripped over a log and sprawled on her face, skinning her hands and knees as she skidded on the rocky ground. "Hans!" she wailed, "I can't run any more!"

"You must keep going!" Jacob screamed at her. "They're right behind us! They'll kill us!" He turned and pushed his way through the bushes toward her.

Hans ran back to his sister, lifted her in his strong arms, then ran with her toward the spot where he had last seen Jacob. He circled behind the bushes, but there was no sign of his Jewish friend. "Jacob," he called softly, "where are you?"

"Down here," came a muffled reply.

Hans set Gretchen on the ground, and then crawled backwards into the bushes, dragging his sister with him. He heard the sound of pounding feet and spun around in time to see several soldiers flash by within three meters of the bushes. "Sit still," he whispered into Gretchen's ear. Seconds later, three more Nazis thundered past.

When the soldiers were out of sight, Hans crawled deeper into the bushes, searching for the hole in which Jacob had hidden. He parted the leafy tendrils of a vine to find a jagged opening in the earth less than a meter long.

He lay on his belly, leaned his face into the hole and whispered, "Jacob, are you down there?"

"*Ja,* right here," came the muffled reply.

"Are you all right?"

"*Ja.* Where are the soldiers?"

"They just ran by," Hans answered, "but I'm sure they're coming back."

"Come down with me. Be quick."

"How deep is it?" Hans asked. "I can't see you."

"About three meters," Jacob replied. "Bring Gretchen quickly. Lower her to me, and I will help her down."

Hans looked up to realize that Gretchen was right beside him. "Hurry," he whispered. "Into the hole. The soldiers will be coming back."

She nodded, dropped her legs into the crevice, and then slowly lowered herself in with her arms braced against each side of the hole. Jacob grabbed her feet and guided her to footholds in the rocks below. Her brother quickly followed.

Hans found himself standing in a narrow cavern. As his eyes grew accustomed to the darkness, he saw a small stream trickling across the rocky floor of the cavern and disappearing under rocks at the lower end of the room. In the other direction, the room stretched for some distance, fading into dark oblivion.

"It's the perfect hiding place," Jacob whispered excitedly.

They froze in silence as they heard the soldiers above them. The Nazis were beating the bushes, shouting, and firing their weapons in an attempt to startle them from their hiding place.

ESCAPE TO LIECHTENSTEIN

"Sit still," Hans whispered to Gretchen. "I don't think they'll find us here."

The clamor died down as the soldiers moved farther into the woods. Jacob sat down beside his two friends. "They won't find us here as long as we stay put," he whispered, "unless they bring dogs in to track us down." He looked at Hans. "How much food do you have?"

Hans knelt on the cave floor, then opened his shirt and carefully let the contents spill out into the sand. "Six carrots, two rutabagas, and some smashed endive," he reported.

Jacob nodded. "The Nazis will be searching these woods for the next two or three days," he said. "We have water here, and if we eat the bare minimum, we can stretch the food for three days. I think we need to stay here for as long as we can."

Hans nodded in agreement. "You won't get any argument from me," he whispered. "I thought we'd had it for sure back there."

Hans stood to his feet and led Gretchen over to the trickling stream. They crouched beside the water while he helped her wash the blood from her skinned hands and knees. *"Danke schön,"* she whispered as they finished. She threw her arms around his neck. "I'm afraid, Hans."

He stroked her blond hair. "God is with us," he said softly. "We have to trust the Lord."

They tiptoed across the narrow grotto and sat down on a limestone ledge across from Jacob. The Jewish boy leaned forward. "I-I want to say something," he said nervously.

Hans and Gretchen turned to him. "Sure, Jacob," Hans whispered. "What is it?"

"I-I want to . . ." He stopped, biting his lip nervously.

Gretchen and Hans sat quietly, waiting expectantly. Jacob looked at the floor of the cavern, wringing his hands anxiously. His face was pale, and his lips trembled. He took a deep breath, expelled it slowly, but still could not bring himself to speak. Hans frowned. What was troubling Jacob so?

"I-I want to ask J-Jesus to save m-me!" Jacob finally blurted. "I know I'm not ready to die, and I'm not going to say *nein* to Him any longer." He looked at Gretchen. "I've been thinking a lot about what you told me the other day when Hans was sick. I am a Jew, and my people do not believe in Jesus Christ. This is very hard for me to do, but I want to ask Jesus to be my Messiah and Savior."

Hans felt warm and happy inside as he said, "Then why don't you do it right now? Are you willing to confess to God that you are a sinner and ask Him for forgiveness?"

The Jewish boy nodded.

"Do you believe that Jesus was the Christ, the Son of God? Do you believe that He died on Calvary for your sins, and that He rose from the grave the third day?"

Jacob nodded again. "*Ja,* I do believe," he replied softly.

"Then why not pray right now," Hans continued, "and ask Jesus to save you? The Bible says, 'For whosoever shall call upon the name of the Lord shall be saved.' Jesus Christ will save you right now if you ask Him."

A huge smile brightened Jacob's thin face as he replied, "*Ja!* I will do it right now!"

ESCAPE TO LIECHTENSTEIN

The three tired, frightened fugitives knelt beside a subterranean stream while the young Jewish boy received Christ as his Savior and Messiah. Jacob prayed haltingly, "Jesus, I have been taught that you were a traitor to my people, but I no longer believe that. I believe that you are the Son of God, and that you died for me. I ask you to be my Savior and forgive all my sins. *Danke schön,* Jesus."

As he looked up, Gretchen startled him by grabbing him in a fierce hug. "Now you're a Christian, Jacob!" she rejoiced.

He nodded happily. "*Ja,* I guess I am."

A few minutes later, Hans climbed the rock wall to the cave's mouth and cautiously stuck his head out. "It's completely dark out," he reported in a whisper when he joined the others. "The Nazis won't be searching anymore tonight."

They stretched out on the cavern floor for the night. The limestone was hard and unyielding, and the cavern was chilly. Huddling together for warmth, they drifted off to sleep, exhausted from the day of terror.

Hans and Jacob awoke at nearly the same instant. They both sat up, stretched, then stood to their feet. Gretchen lay sleeping, curled up in a fetal position. "Let her sleep," Jacob whispered, and Hans nodded.

Be with us, Lord Jesus, Hans prayed silently as he gazed down at the sleeping form of his sister. *Help us get safely to the border. I'm doing my best to take care of Gretchen, but what can I do if the Nazis capture us? Please, watch over my little sister! And help me to trust You. My faith is so weak!*

Hans watched as Jacob climbed to the cavern entrance. Jacob cautiously poked his head out and then stood quietly surveying the woods around them. Finally, he returned to the cavern floor. "All's quiet out there," he whispered. "But I'm sure they'll be scouring these woods all day. We don't dare venture outside, but I think we're safe here."

Hans nodded in agreement.

Jacob suddenly grinned. "In a time like this, it's *gut* to be a Christian, *ja?*"

Hans smiled at him. *"Ja,"* he answered. "I'm glad that you received Jesus yesterday."

Gretchen stirred, opened her eyes, and sat up. "I'm hungry," she announced. "Let's eat."

"There's one carrot apiece today," her brother told her. "I don't know about you, but I'm going to wait until later to eat mine."

"I want mine now," Gretchen announced.

"Fine," Hans replied, "but remember, there's nothing later on." He handed her a carrot.

The girl began to nibble slowly at the vegetable. "I'm going to eat just a little of it now," she said.

Jacob suddenly held up one hand. "Sh-h!" he hissed. "Listen!"

Overhead, the thud of running feet echoed down through the earth. The soldiers had returned. Hans, Gretchen, and Jacob sat quietly listening as the Nazi troops searched the woods for them.

"I-I'm afraid," Gretchen whispered.

Jacob leaned forward. "They won't find us in here," he reassured her. "The entrance to this cave is too well hidden."

Hans sat down beside her. "Trust in Jesus, Gretchen," he said tenderly. "Remember what David said in the book of Psalms? 'What time I am afraid, I will trust in thee.' David wrote that when he was hiding from King Saul."

She looked up at him, and her face suddenly brightened. "I remember that story from the Bible," she replied. "David hid in a cave several times, didn't he? Just like us."

Jacob came over and crouched on a rock beside them. "Does God know that we're down here?" he asked quietly.

"*Ja*, He does!" Hans replied. "He's watching over us right now, just like He did for David."

The noise overhead subsided as the soldiers worked their way through the forest, and the young people relaxed. Jacob stood up and stretched. "It's going to be a long day," he whispered.

Suddenly, he stiffened. A new sound rang out through the woods, bringing a chill of fear to the three young people. They heard the distinct baying of hounds following a trail!

"They brought the dogs," Jacob groaned. "They have bloodhounds on our trail."

"Will they find us?" Gretchen worried, cupping her hands to her mouth.

Jacob nodded. "The hounds will lead the Nazis right to us," he replied. "There's no escape."

"What can we do?" Hans wondered aloud.

Jacob shrugged. "I don't know," he answered. "We don't dare leave the cave, but the hounds will bring the soldiers right to us if we stay here. We're lost either way."

"We could hide farther back in the cave," Gretchen suggested. "I've heard that caves like this can go for miles under the earth."

Hans shook his head. "We don't dare risk it," he replied. "We have no lights, and there could be drop-offs. The soldiers can bring searchlights, and they would still find us. I don't know what to do."

Just then, a hound bayed loudly. The sound came from just outside their hiding place. A strange, sniffling sound suddenly caught their attention, and they all looked up to see the ugly, mournful face of a hound appear overhead in the cave entrance. The dogs had found them!

Gretchen, Hans, and Jacob crouched in fear, waiting for the Nazis to call them out of hiding. But no soldiers came. The big dog snuffled and whined as he watched the three young people below.

Suddenly, Jacob sprang to his feet. "This dog outran the pack," he said in excitement. "The soldiers were too far behind him! Let's see if he's friendly."

He scrambled up the rock wall toward the hound, and the dog whined eagerly as he approached. He reached up and petted the dog's head, then scratched his ears. "Come on," he called to the others. "He's friendly. Let's get out of here. We'll take him with us."

Speechless with amazement, Hans and Gretchen quickly followed their friend from the cave. When they crawled from the bushes, they found Jacob petting and hugging the hound, who wagged his long tail in frenzied pleasure. "Come on," he called when he saw them. "Let's get out of here!" He whistled to the dog. "Here, boy."

They hurried down the shady trail through the woods, the big hound trotting eagerly behind them. "It's still nearly sixty kilometers to the border," Jacob called over his shoulder. "We don't stand a chance, but we can sure try."

His enthusiasm died suddenly. Two soldiers with automatic rifles sprang from the bushes and blocked the trail!

ESCAPE TO LIECHTENSTEIN

One soldier covered them with his rifle while the other bound their hands tightly behind them, then looped a length of rope through their arms, binding them together. The hound sat quietly, his doleful eyes watching sadly as the three were bound.

The soldier with the rifle walked forward and jerked the kerchief from Jacob's head. "It's the Jew boy!" he said, laughing. "We got what we came for!"

The soldiers prodded the three captives back down the trail with their rifles. Hans, Gretchen, and Jacob stared at each other in dismay. The Nazis had captured them! Hans trembled as he realized that all three of them were facing certain death.

CHAPTER NINETEEN
THE NAZI COLONEL

The Nazi truck bounced and rattled as it sped along over the rough road. The three captives lay tightly bound on the cold steel floor of the vehicle, wincing at each bump. The two stern-faced soldiers, rifles in hand, sat on the wooden benches that ran along the sides of the truck.

"What's going to happen now?" Gretchen wailed.

"Silence!" one of the soldiers snarled, kicking her in the back.

Hans gritted his teeth in frustration, realizing that he was powerless to do anything to help his sister. Jacob, however, had ideas of his own. Rolling over on his back, he raised both legs high in the air and aimed a kick at the soldier.

The Nazi saw it coming and simply swung his own legs to one side. He cocked his rifle, raised it to his cheek, and sighted in on Jacob's head. "Try it again, Jew boy," he taunted. "I'll be glad to pull the trigger." Jacob lay still, knowing that the man meant every word.

After half an hour of the torturous ride, the truck slowed for a turn, then accelerated to climb a hill. The driver braked so abruptly that the captives slid forward, slamming into each other. One of the soldiers riding in back dropped the tailgate, then motioned for the captives to get out. "Come," he ordered. "Quickly!"

They struggled to their feet and stumbled to the back of the truck. One of the soldiers took the rope off that tied them together and assisted Gretchen and Hans as they climbed down. Then he reached up to help Jacob. As Jacob leaned forward, the Nazi suddenly let him go, allowing him to fall from the tailgate. He struck the ground hard, unable to break his fall since his hands were tied behind him.

"What's the matter, Jew boy?" the soldier taunted. "Lose your balance?"

Jacob scrambled to his feet, his teeth clenched in an attempt to hide the pain in his shoulder. He stood quietly with Hans and Gretchen, his face showing no emotion. The soldier grinned and turned away.

They were marched up the hill toward a three-story brick building shaded by tall elms. A huge Nazi flag hung vertically over the doorway, and Gretchen shuddered as they passed beneath it.

Their guards led them quickly up a flight of stairs, then down a long hallway of locked doors. Pausing before a door, one man selected a key from a large ring, unlocked the door, then thrust them inside.

"You'll stay here until the Gestapo calls for you," he said, and then the door thudded shut. The deadbolt slammed home, and the sound reverberated through the room.

Gretchen sank to the floor and began to weep softly. Jacob paced back and forth, clasping and unclasping his hands. Hans watched them both for a moment and attempted a smile. "Look on the bright side," he said, doing his best to sound cheerful. "We're twenty or thirty kilometers closer to the border now, and we didn't even have to walk it!"

Jacob glared at him. "Don't you understand? We're as good as dead! Even God can't help us now."

Hans shrugged. "He's done it before, hasn't He?" he replied. "Several times. How do you think we found the beaver den? How do you think you stumbled into that cave last night?"

"Well, it was all for nothing," Jacob shot back. "We're in the hands of the Nazis now! All our running was for nothing."

"Maybe not," the other answered. "God still wants us to trust Him, and He can get us out of here if He wills."

Hans looked around the little room. A grid of steel bars covered the one window high overhead, but it admitted a fair amount of light. A naked light bulb hung over the empty cell on a snake-like length of black wire. Every sound echoed harshly off the dull cement walls and dirty floor.

Jacob sank to the floor in discouragement beside Gretchen, but Hans explored every inch of their prison, searching for a way of escape. The window was too high and too small, and besides, it was securely barred. The steel door was dead bolted. He knew immediately that it was no use even trying to pick the lock. There had to be another way. And then, his eyes fell on a small vent on the wall.

"Jacob," he whispered excitedly, "help me get this grating loose from this vent! It may be the way out of here!"

Jacob shrugged. "It's no use," he said despondently. "We don't even know that it leads anywhere."

"*Ja,* but we've got to try," Hans insisted. "It's the only possible way out. I've already checked the door and the window."

"*Nein,*" the Jewish boy replied. "It's no use."

Hans was upset. "You can't just lie down and quit!" he exploded. He lowered his voice. "What about Major Von Bronne? What about the documents? What's going to happen to them?"

Frowning, Jacob stood to his feet. "Well, it's worth a try."

Gretchen suddenly jumped up with a triumphant smile on her face. "Look," she whispered excitedly. "My hands are free!"

Hans and Jacob stared at her in amazement. "How did you do that?" her brother asked.

"I just twisted and twisted until the ropes were loose enough to untie," Gretchen answered. "Let me see if I can untie yours." The boys' hands were tied more tightly, but in a few minutes she had them both free.

Hans laughed. "*Danke schön,* Gretchen. That was good work for a girl!"

He rubbed his wrists as he studied the vent. "There are only four screws holding it in place," he observed. "If we can take those out, it ought to come free." He searched his pockets. "I don't have a thing to use as a screwdriver," he said. "Have you got a knife?"

Jacob shook his head. "*Nein.* But there's got to be something we can use! Maybe we can pull the whole thing right out of the wall. Here, let's try together."

Hans gripped the vent with both hands, pleased that some of the Jewish boy's old spirit was returning. They strained and pulled, but the grating refused to budge. "Let's try again." Jacob urged. "It's got to give."

Finally, breathing hard, they sank to the floor in defeat. "What do we do now?" Hans groaned.

"There's got to be something in this room that we can use for a screwdriver," Jacob said. "Let's see what we can find."

They searched the room again and even went through their pockets, but they found nothing. Hans's eyes went to Jacob's boots, and suddenly he had an idea. "Hey!" he whispered, "you could use one of the eyelets from your boots!"

Jacob unlaced one of his boots, then spent the next thirty minutes working one of the metal eyelets loose from the tough leather. When it finally came free, he straightened the hook by prying it against one corner of the vent grating. He held the object up for Hans's inspection. "What do you think?"

Hans nodded. "*Ja,* it might work. Just try not to bend it."

Jacob knelt in front of the vent and inserted the edge of the makeshift tool into the slot of one screw. Clenching his teeth in concentration, he pushed hard against the metal eyelet and twisted it counterclockwise. "The screw moved," Hans whispered. "Try again."

Gretchen came over to watch. Jacob tried again. This time, the screw moved a little more. On the third try, the screw began to turn freely. The second screw came out easily enough, and on the third, the eyelet broke. Jacob spent another twenty minutes fashioning another screwdriver from a second eyelet. Carefully, he removed the two remaining screws.

"All right," Hans said excitedly. "Let's see if it will come free. Ready? Pull!"

They tugged together at the grating, and to their immense satisfaction, it slid easily from the wall. They still had it in their hands when the door suddenly opened, and the two Nazi soldiers burst into the room.

"So," one soldier snarled, "trying to escape, *ja?*" He strode across the room and kicked the grating with such force that it flew from their hands, careened off the wall, and landed with a clatter on the floor behind them. Hans's wrist was gashed by the sharp metal edge.

ESCAPE TO LIECHTENSTEIN

The man was furious when he realized that their hands were untied. He retrieved the lengths of rope from the floor, grabbed Hans by the wrists, and forced his hands behind his back. As he retied the boy's hands, he jerked his arms up painfully, tying the knots so tightly that the ropes bit deeply into the flesh. Hans's hands began to tingle as he watched the Nazi tie Gretchen and Jacob. For some unknown reason, the man tied Gretchen's hands in front.

Hans realized that his circulation was being cut off, but he knew better than to ask the soldier to loosen his bonds. *Lord, help us,* he prayed silently.

When all three captives had been retied, the soldier prodded them roughly toward the door where the second soldier waited. "You three are to be given a free trip to Berlin," the second Nazi told them, "courtesy of the Gestapo! But first, the Colonel wants to see you. He'll be here soon."

They were led into an office with a huge mahogany desk in the center of a thick cream-colored rug. A huge Nazi flag adorned the wall behind the desk, and beneath it hung several framed photographs of Hitler himself in full dress uniform. Four leather armchairs lined one wall, and their captors indicated that they were to be seated. The two soldiers stood leaning against the wall opposite them, the butts of their rifles resting on the rug.

As Hans sank into the deep comfort of the chair, he felt a tremendous weight of fear upon his chest. He could hardly breathe. *We'll soon come face to face with the Nazi officer who will decide our fate. Will we be tortured before being shot? Will we have the fortitude to keep from revealing the existence of the secret documents?*

He glanced at Gretchen and knew immediately that she was experiencing the same feelings. Her head was down, and her face was pale. She clenched her fists tightly in front of her chest, as though to protect herself. *God, help us!* Hans prayed desperately. *Watch over Gretchen!*

The door opened suddenly, and three Nazi officers strode in. Two lieutenants flanked the colonel, a tall, beefy man with a red face and graying hair. He exuded authority, and his very presence seemed to electrify the room. The soldiers stood stiffly at attention as the three officers entered.

"Ah," the dignified colonel said in satisfaction as he studied the worried faces of the three captives. He rubbed his hands together in anticipation. "The three little foxes have finally been brought to bay by the Nazi hounds, *ja?*" He laughed, and a chill of horror swept over Hans. "Do you know how much trouble you have caused us? But we have you now!"

Jacob leaped to his feet. "Major, we—"

"Silence!" the Nazi officer roared.

"But Herr Major, I—"

The big officer's hand shot out, gripping Jacob by the front of his shirt and lifting his thin frame from the floor. He shook the Jewish boy violently, as effortlessly as a cat shakes a rat. He lowered his huge hand, allowing Jacob to fall back into his chair. "You'll not speak unless you are spoken to!" he thundered. Jacob sagged limply against the back of the chair.

"Krause!"

One of the lieutenants stepped forward quickly. *"Ja!"*

"Krause, I'm authorizing an extra week's pay for these two grenadiers. Write a commendation for each of them and have it on my desk to sign tomorrow morning. See to it immediately."

The lieutenant saluted, and the colonel turned to the two soldiers. "*Gut* work, men," he said, saluting each man, who returned his salute smartly. "The Third Reich is indebted to you! Dismissed!"

The soldiers followed Lieutenant Krause out the door. The stern-faced colonel watched the door close behind them, then turned to face Jacob. "Tell me," he demanded, "where are the documents?"

CHAPTER TWENTY
ENCOUNTER AT THE BORDER

The lieutenant stepped forward and quickly untied each of the three young captives. They sat silently, rubbing their chafed wrists gingerly. The colonel drew up the fourth chair, sat down facing them and leaned forward intently. "Where are the documents?" he asked again.

Hans and Gretchen watched in horror as Jacob leaned over and began to unlace his right boot. "*Nein,* Jacob!" Hans called out. "*Nein!* Think of Austria!"

The Jewish boy straightened up and stared at his friend, then a slow smile spread across his face. "Don't you understand?" he asked. "This is the man Papa told me to give the documents to. This is Major Von Bronne!"

Startled, Hans and Gretchen stared at the officer. "Major Von Bronne?" Hans echoed. "You mean we . . . this . . . this is the major? He's on our side?"

Jacob nodded happily. "This is the major," he replied.

Hans let out a whoop of joy. "God did it!" He laughed. "Didn't I tell you? God took care of us! He led us right to the major." He suddenly looked crestfallen. "We never should have doubted Him."

The big man laughed, then said, "It's Colonel Von Bronne now, Jacob. I've been promoted. It's a good thing you ended up here too," he said seriously. "The Gestapo has plans for you three in Berlin. I'll spare you the details, but I assure you that they weren't pleasant. Gestapo agents are planning to pick you up this evening to begin your trip. But they won't find you here. I will escort you across the border personally in my automobile."

"I saw the major—uh, the colonel with Papa once," Jacob explained. "So I recognized him as soon as he walked into the room."

"Sorry I had to rough you up a bit," the officer apologized, "but it had to look good for Lieutenant Krause and the two grenadiers. I hope I didn't hurt you."

Jacob shook his head. "*Nein,* I'm all right."

Colonel Von Bronne gestured toward the other officer. "This is Lieutenant Hofer," he said. "He can be trusted. He is one of us."

Jacob nodded. "And this is Hans Kaltenbrunner and his sister Gretchen," he replied. "I owe my life to them!"

The officers shook hands with Gretchen and Hans. "*Gut* to have you on our side," Colonel Von Bronne said with a friendly grin. "You two have performed an outstanding service for your country. I am grateful for your loyalty to Austria."

Jacob bent down and continued to unlace his boot. "The documents are safe," he told the officer, his eyes sparkling with pride. "Papa sewed them into the linings of my boots. I have them all."

The Colonel waved his hand. "Then leave them there," he ordered. "Your boots will be the safest place for them until we get to Liechtenstein."

He looked over at his lieutenant. "We must leave quickly," he said. "Have preparations been made?"

Lieutenant Hofer saluted. "All is ready."

Jacob retied his boot. "What about Papa?" he asked anxiously. "Did he make it? Have you heard from him?"

The big officer smiled broadly. "He is all right," he told the boy. "He is safe in Switzerland. But he has been very concerned for your safety." He pulled a gold watch from his pocket and glanced at it. "You will see him soon," he promised. "We will leave shortly."

Gretchen leaned forward, brushing her hair from her face. "What about us?" she worried. "What will we do?"

"You will come with us," the Colonel replied. "We will take you to Switzerland. You are no longer safe in Austria."

"But what about Papa?" the girl asked. "How will he know where we are?"

Colonel Von Bronne frowned. "Who is your father?" he asked. "Where could we find him?"

"He's in the German army," Hans answered, "but he is a loyal Austrian! He was made to serve against his wishes."

The colonel nodded. "I understand. How would we find him? Do you have any idea where he was stationed?"

Hans shook his head. *"Nein,"* he answered, "but his name is Hans Kaltenbrunner, same as mine."

"It will not be easy to find him, but we will do our best," Colonel Von Bronne promised. "His life will be in danger once the Nazis know your identity and trace you to him."

He looked from one worried face to another. "But don't be alarmed," he said kindly. "Our men will find him. I am an Allied agent," he explained. "But now that we have found you, we must leave Austria tonight. Once it is known that I have helped you escape, I will be as hot as you three. But we have other agents who will search for your father."

ESCAPE TO LIECHTENSTEIN

Lieutenant Hofer strode to the window, peered outside, and then let the drapes drop back into place. "It is growing dark, sir," he reported. "I will prepare the automobile."

Colonel Von Bronne nodded. "Very well," he replied. "We will leave in twenty minutes."

The shiny black limousine sped along the dark, narrow road, the beams from its headlights illuminating the huge rain drops that angled across the road. A brilliant flash of lightning split the sky, followed by the booming voice of thunder. The clouds suddenly unleashed a torrent of rain, and the struggling windshield wipers could not keep up. Lieutenant Hofer crouched over the wheel, wiping the fogging windshield with a handkerchief. "We're about ten kilometers from the border, sir," he reported.

Colonel Von Bronne, seated in the luxurious back seat between Gretchen and Hans, nodded in approval. "Very well." He leaned forward and placed a hand on the shoulder of Jacob, who was seated on the front seat beside the lieutenant. "You'll see your father soon, Jacob."

The boy looked over his shoulder at the Colonel. *"Danke schön,"* he said quietly. "I am eager." Suddenly his eyes widened in alarm. "Colonel—behind us! We are being followed!"

Colonel Von Bronne turned slowly and glanced out the back window. Two pairs of headlights swept around the curve behind, illuminating the trees flanking the road. *"Ja,* so we are," he observed calmly. "Lieutenant Krause was on to us, after all. He has alerted the Gestapo!" He leaned forward. "Hofer! Step on it!"

The lieutenant tromped on the accelerator, and the limousine shot forward. Gretchen and Hans turned to watch the headlights behind them and were dismayed to see that the other vehicles were still gaining. *"Ja,* they are following us, all right," Hans said.

At that moment, he saw flashes of gunfire, and the glass of the back window shattered as bullets thudded into it. The occupants of the limousine dropped to the floor, and the lieutenant hunched even lower over the wheel. A machine gun chattered behind them, and a shower of glass rained in on the back seat as the window disintegrated. Gretchen flinched as a jagged shard of flying glass struck her cheek, leaving a nasty gash. Hans held a piece of cloth to her face to stop the bleeding, unaware that he also had sustained several minor cuts.

Colonel Von Bronne drew a shiny automatic from his belt, knelt on the back seat, then popped up in the back window, firing at the vehicles behind them. His fifth shot found its mark. One of the front tires on the leading vehicle suddenly blew out, and the automobile skidded sideways across the road just as the limousine flashed across a small iron bridge spanning a tiny creek. The driver of the second vehicle did not brake in time, and his auto slammed into the side of the first.

"That will buy us a little time," Colonel Von Bronne said, holstering his weapon. "How far are we from the border?"

"It's just ahead," the lieutenant answered. "Unless they've got road blocks up, we'll be across in five minutes!"

Moments later, the speeding limousine swung around a gentle curve, and the Austrian-Liechtenstein border loomed just ahead. "We made it," Jacob cried. "*Danke schön,* Lord Jesus!"

The headlights illuminated a two-lane steel bridge spanning the Samina River. There were tall steel fences topped with barbed wire stretching in both directions along the Austrian bank. A black-and-white barrier blocked the approach to the bridge, and a lone Nazi soldier stood guard, his machine gun cradled across his chest.

The limousine slowed slightly. "Colonel," Lieutenant Hofer called, "do I ram him?"

"Nein!" the colonel replied. "Stop the auto. We will talk our way across."

The rear of the limousine fishtailed dangerously on the wet pavement as the lieutenant hastily applied the brakes. The vehicle skidded to a stop less than ten meters from the startled guard. He approached the driver's side of the limousine, his machine gun leveled at the car. Lieutenant Hofer rolled down the window.

The Nazi soldier's helmet streamed water from the pelting rain as he took one hand from his machine gun just long enough for a hasty salute, then gripped the weapon again with both hands. "I must see your papers," he said.

Gretchen stared in astonishment. Her mouth fell open; she attempted to speak, but no words came out. Finally, she found her voice. "Papa!" she cried. "Hans! It's Papa!"

Hans stared at the soldier in disbelief, then turned to the German officer in the seat beside him. "Colonel," he stammered. "This is our father!"

The limousine swiftly left the Liechtenstein border behind and accelerated up the steep Swiss mountain road. In the back of the vehicle, a man in a Nazi uniform lay back against the seat, his wet uniform soaking the plush fabric. His strong right arm was around the shoulder of a grinning young boy, while his left hand stroked the blond braids of the tearful, young girl who leaned her head against his shoulder.

"Oh, Papa," the girl sighed again, "you don't know how happy we are to see you!"

Herr Kaltenbrunner grinned and drew his daughter closer. "God was watching over all of us, my love," he said softly.

In the front seat, Colonel Von Bronne turned to the young Jewish boy beside him. "We'll be in Altdorf in less than two hours," he said. "Your father will be delighted to see you."

He glanced toward the back seat. "You three have been through a lot, I know," he said softly. "But what you have done may very well change the whole course of the war. Austria has three new heroes!"

Herr Kaltenbrunner spoke up. "Here's one man that's proud of them," he said. He hugged Hans and Gretchen even tighter.

Hans smiled modestly. "You know, it's really amazing the way the Lord worked this all out for us," he commented.

"The Lord does that for those who love Him," his father replied.

"I know," Hans said, "but it still was amazing. The Nazis who captured us brought us to Colonel Von Bronne, the one officer who could help us. Any others would have turned us over to the Gestapo. The papers would have been back in Nazi hands, and we would have been killed. And then, you just happened to be stationed at the bridge we crossed!"

"I know you went through quite an ordeal these last few days," Herr Kaltenbrunner said, "but it's obvious that the Lord had the details all planned out before you even started out."

"Best of all," Gretchen chimed in, "Jacob got saved! God must have planned for him to come right to our barn, so that we could travel with him." In the front seat, Jacob smiled in agreement.

Hans began to recount for his father all the adventures that they had been through, beginning with the Nazi raid on Mittersill and the search for Jacob. Herr Kaltenbrunner listened eagerly, expressing amazement from time to time. Hans glanced over at Gretchen and smiled at what he saw. His sister was snuggled up against her father, her blond head resting on his shoulder, her eyes closed. The long day had completely worn her out.

ESCAPE TO LIECHTENSTEIN

But as Hans continued to talk, his own eyelids began to grow heavy. The hum of the automobile motor was hypnotizing. In minutes, he also was asleep.

Glossary

ankerbrot (**ang**·ker·broht) white Austrian bread

Anschluss (**an**·schloos) the forced union of Austria with Germany by Hitler in 1938

auf wiedersehen (owf **vee**·der·zayn) good-bye

danke schön (**dahn**·kuh shayn) many thanks

dirndl (**dirn**·del) Austrian peasant dress with bodice laced up the front

Frau (frauw) Mrs.

Fräulein (**froy**·lyn) lady, or Miss

führer (**few**·rohr) reference to Adolf Hitler, leader of the Nazi party

Gestapo (**ge**·stop·o) the German military police

gulasch (**goo**·lush) Austrian stew

gulyassuppe (**goo**·ea·**zoo**·peh) a goulash soup of Hungarian origin

gut (goot) good

guten morgen (goot·uhn **mawr**·guhn) good morning

guten tag (goot·uhn **tahg**) good day, how do you do?

Herr (Hehr) Mr.

ja (yah) yes

knabe (**knah**·buh) boy

leberknodlsuppe (**leh**·behr·**noydl**·zooh·peh) meat broth with round dumplings

Luftwaffe (**luft**·vahf) Nazi air strikes

Nazi (**naht**·zee) Adolf Hitler's German political party

nein (nyn) no

panzer (**pan**·zer) a German tank

Reich (righk) used with "Third" to refer to the Third Power—Nazism

schoeberl (**she**·beryl) fried pancake

simonbrot (**zym**·uhn·broht) black bread

swastika (**svah**·stick·ah) entwined broken crosses; emblem of the Nazi regime

tafelspitz (**tuh**·fill·shpits) boiled beef, an Austrian favorite

tellerminen (**tell**·or·myn·uhn) dish-shaped German land mine

unteroffizier (**untr**·off·fits·eer) German officer, equivalent of sergeant